For T, J and D
It's always all for you.

Lady Mafia

MEMBERSHIP

THIS CERTIFICATE IS PROUDLY AWARDED TO
BAD ASS :

ALL MEMBERSHIPS MUST REMAIN SECRET

Zinny
ZINNY
Ceo

Indy
INDY
CEO

xo aster ♡
ASTER
CEO

Lady MAFIA

DEBRA
USA Today Bestselling Author
ANASTASIA

CHAPTER
ONE

The three women that we were looking for at the airport should not have stood out. They were supposed to be professionals. Three of the smartest women in the world. Risky, brave, and deadly.

We weren't the only ones looking for them. The Kaleotos wanted them. The Syndicate was looking for them. Even other criminals wanted them, and certainly wanted the money their capture would bring. I had a different goal. I wanted to save my brother Matt's life. And it was my fault that he was even in trouble.

Max, the crime boss, went by one simple name. Growing up two towns over from Slots, Maryland, allowed me to grow up in a fairly normal situation, but with the temptation of all Slots could offer. My brother liked to gamble. Okay, he loved to gamble. Sometimes he was good at it. Sometimes he was horrible at it. After borrowing too much from a dicey loan shark and defaulting on his loan, Max gave my brother his repayment terms. When Matt failed to make a payment, the burden of his loan shifted to me. I had to head up the crew that was looking for the Lady Mafia, and I had to be successful at finding them or my brother died. The ransom for the Lady Mafia would pay off my brother's debt in full.

Who was I? Well, I worked for the government. That's what most people got out of me when they asked. The reality was where my brother enjoyed taking risks with his money, I enjoyed taking risks with my life. My job was working for a contractor that worked for the military. I specialized in the unspecializable stuff. You needed a document from a heavily guarded facility? They sent me instead of a SWAT team. I'm great with a gun, better with my mouth and quick with my retreat. I think Max messed with my brother just to get to me. Get me in debt to him somehow. And my latest job was my most important.

The Lady Mafia had burned their reputation in the crime world. One minute no one knew of them and then, in the next second, everyone was talking about them.

The rumor was that each of the three women had a piece of intelligence that should fit together like a puzzle. That's all I knew. I needed all three, and I needed them alive. There were a ton of crews that were researching the identities of the Lady Mafia. Most that were in on this job? The worst that could happen to them would be losing out on a huge reward. For me? I was going to lose someone I loved.

After a month of working with my first crew, I had found something that I was hoping everyone else hadn't noticed. There was a hashtag on social media called #LadyMaafia. The girls in the selfies attached matched what we thought we knew about the ladies age wise. This was an enormous risk. A big gamble. We were in the right place. Slots was a smaller version of Las Vegas but with all the same vices available. Their plane finally landed. Now was the moment of truth.

I looked at Tucker as he pointed to the gangway. Three women stumbled into view. They seemed like a cluster of bags, and I was pretty sure that two of them were accidentally tied together with headphones. The brunette had the blonde in a vise grip, her fingertips denting the pale skin.

"How the hell did you find shrimp on the plane? Goddammit, Aster."

Aster responded through her pursed lips—like she was playing that kid game where you pretended to be a fish. "Mhhm. Murrrmhhh. Madu."

"I told you something was up when she was wearing a baggy dress." The redhead disentangled herself from Aster, letting the headphones dangle.

They moved in our direction. I met Tucker's eyes. These were not the women we were looking for.

Before we could say anything, I was eye to eye with the angry, gorgeous brunette. "Do you have any Benadryl?"

I shook my head no, trying to blend into the crowd. I was never supposed to stand out. It was one of my special talents. But either she'd made me or she was desperate for help. I was in deep shit now. Not bringing in the Lady Mafia would get my entire crew out of the running for the money. They didn't know I was planning on swapping the money for my brother and getting the hell out of dodge. I would not pay any of them their fair share. I mean, I would, assuming we all lived through this, mail them their money after I made it. It was basically robbing one to pay the other now.

"I swear to all that is good and holy, that if I find an EpiPen, I'm holding you down and slamming it into your heart."

The brunette turned back to me as if I was part of the conversation. "Do you know what she does? She eats shrimp so she will blow up like a balloon. Have you ever heard of an allergy to shellfish that causes a person to only swell in her tits, ass, and lips?"

The blonde of the unfortunate allergic reaction was wearing a little crown that read, *Bride to Be*. The redhead had on a matching headband that read, *Bride's Bitch*.

"Um. No." I wasn't supposed to talk to the targets, but they weren't supposed to find me first. I had to roll with the punches. These girls were having trouble getting off a plane like three grown ass women. They were not some of the world's most feared assassins.

We needed three women tomorrow. And these women actually had pink satin jackets with *Lady Mafia* emblazoned on the back. I think that made it worse.

This was a case of mistaken identity. I heard Breck in my ear—the wireless communication was hidden. "The plane is empty. These are the girls behind the #LadyMaafia hashtag. It matches with their profile pictures. We're fucked. This is a massive misdirection or..."

"Bad luck and these women are just horrible spellers," I finished for Breck. I had to make some quick decisions. These women needed to come with us on the slim chance that we could make something work. My brother's life depended on it.

Aster's eyes went wide before she looked down at her chest. "Here we go!"

I watched, mesmerized, as her right breast seemed to self-inflate. And then her left breast followed. What had once been excess fabric was now brimming with swollen cleavage.

Breck was in my ear again. "Um, did her boobs just pop up out of nowhere?"

Next, she whirled around and pointed at her rear. It did a similar trick. Her figure went from nice to ridiculous. I felt like I was in a paranormal movie. Nothing on the human body was supposed to change that quickly.

Aster started giggling. "Bang. Pop. I'm here to make it drop." She started twerking with her now bulbous booty.

"And now we have the dancing personality. Shit." The brunette grabbed Aster by the upper arm. "We really needed the chatty Instagram model to celebrate your upcoming wedding?"

Aster tugged on her now painted-on dress. "This dress was on clearance! What was I supposed to do, Indy?"

Indy, the brunette, grabbed up all of Aster's bags and fashioned a quick hand leash out of Aster's headphones and used it to drag her farther into the airport.

I decided. "We keep them until we know. Lev, you in place?"

"Yeah, boss. I'm out here in the fake Uber waiting on a really stacked shrimp addict and a mad chick."

I couldn't believe I was uttering these words on the job, "They all have tiaras on."

"Copy that. Girls in tiaras."

There was a crackle in my ear as the connection in our wireless earpieces shifted.

We were going to have to kidnap three drunk women, one of whom was apparently in anaphylactic shock, in broad daylight. This day had gone from shit to super utter shit.

CHAPTER
TWO

I was sick of it. Sick of Aster making herself sick to fit an ideal that only her fiancé saw. I glanced over at Zinny. She had the same look of frustration on her face that I felt in my heart.

These two women were my family. We'd been together longer than we'd done anything else in life.

The hot piece of suit that I had vented to was trailing behind us. Zinny pointed at the car/taxi signs, and we walked as quickly as we could. Aster was stumbling, and I slowed a bit. We needed an antihistamine quickly. Exercise would only exacerbate the poison that Aster had willingly taken.

I looked at Aster again. Her lips looked painful. The men walking past us were taking more notice the bigger her erogenous zones got.

I felt a tap on my shoulder and whirled around. The hot piece of suit held out an EpiPen.

"You needed this? For that... situation?" He gestured to Aster's ginormous tits and ass.

I gripped the pen and pulled the blue safety off with my teeth. I bent Aster over and embedded the pen into her thigh for a count of three.

When I pulled out the pen, I twirled it and handed it back to the hot suit guy. "Can you find a place to put this sharp? And thanks. You saved her life."

I threaded my fingers in Aster's hair and pulled her up to standing. I forced her to look at me. "You good?" Her color was a little better already. God bless EpiPens.

"You know, if you scramble the letters, EpiPens would be penis pe," Aster offered.

"I'm going to get us on the next flight home. Enough of this bachelorette party. You suck." We'd have to get to a ticket counter.

Zinny was already flashing the Dansett Air app at me, clearly thinking the same thing. "The flights are full. And she should rest."

I still had a zoomy buzz from the drinks on the plane, so I nodded.

"Guys, please. This is my last night to party. I'm locking it down. We have so many plans. The casino. The Flirty Jones concert. We have that grand suite. Please? The last hurrah! The three Bust-keteers take one last ride." Her eyes filled up. She really wanted this. "You, me, and Zinny forever."

I shook my head. "This is against my better judgment."

We were causing a scene. Well, Aster always did when she was puffed up like a sex doll. But even above and beyond that, we had to move. We were blocking the flow of people.

Aster put her hands together as if she were praying. "Please. So, so please. You're the prettiest and the smartest and I love you."

I rolled my eyes but nodded. She squealed and jumped up and down. Everything she had jiggled. The surrounding men looked hypnotized. "Let's go get an Uber."

Zinny looped her arm through Aster's elbow and helped me steer her to the cars and bus exit. We were doing this thing. Aster had, unfortunately, tons of experience with the shrimp. Her fiancé insisted on it, claiming he couldn't get it up if she wasn't the overblown version of herself.

Zinny and I were not fans at all, but Aster insisted he was worth it. That going through this was worth it.

Hot Suit was still a few steps behind us. "Hey, just want to make sure you ladies get in your car okay. There are a lot of guys kind of following."

He wasn't wrong.

"Nice to run into a gentleman."

I could swear his right eye twitched. His hickory eyes had a deeper brown ring closer to his pupils. He was really, really good-looking, but those eyes seemed like I was looking into a painting of the galaxy. Mesmerizing.

We made it to the Uber, bags stuffed in the trunk before I found out that hot piece of suit with the nice eyes was anything but a gentleman.

CHAPTER
THREE

T hey were impaired, so joining the ladies in the back seat of the black SUV Lev was driving was a simple move. Lev hit the door locks. I pulled out my pistol and let it lay on my lap.

Indy cuddled Aster to her bosom and fumed in my direction. Zinny, the annoyed redhead, was thoroughly confused.

"Wait, what? Why is the airport guy in here?"

Indy lifted her eyebrows after taking in my gun. "Something sinister going on here, Hot Suit?"

I felt uncomfortable under her disappointed gaze.

"Listen, we just need to borrow you ladies for a few hours. Then we can drop you off at the airport." I held my hands out, palms up. "Just stay calm."

Aster's eyes grew wide, as if they were part of her allergic reaction, too. And the noise she started making in her chest was as close to a fire truck I'd ever heard a human make. "Wearegoingto-DIEEEEEEE!"

She began flailing her arms. Her boobs came dangerously close to popping out of her skintight strapless dress.

"Just do as we tell you and no one gets hurt," I offered the cliche line when Aster took a deep breath.

"Oh, my sweet baby Jesus in a bassinet near a newborn kitten. He said the thing. The thing they say in all the movies. Holy crap. Bury me in my wedding dress. Shit. We're all going to die. No one will know my wishes. I have to text Spenser. He needs to know."

She pulled her phone from out of the front of her dress. Where in the world she was keeping the huge cell phone, I wasn't sure. But as she started thumbing a text, I snapped to my senses and confiscated her phone and asked for the other two to cough theirs up as well.

Zinny threw hers at me, but luckily I caught it before it hit me in the nuts.

She hissed at me. Indy held hers out to me but pulled on it when I tried to take it. "Your mom proud of you? This what she always dreamed for her son?"

I didn't answer but had to swallow a helping of guilt. Then she let go of her phone, cuddling Aster again, smoothing out her hair. "Don't cry, baby. He got us the EpiPen, so he can't be completely evil."

Lev, from the driver's seat, didn't help. "Well, we need you alive. All of you."

"Hey!" I admonished him and slapped his headrest. "Professionalism here. Let's not tip our hand."

"What? We're dead anyway. These girls aren't the professional killers we need. They barely qualify as functioning adults." Lev punched his steering wheel, making Aster gasp.

Indy patted Aster's back. "It's going to be okay. As soon as our buzz fades, we'll make some sense out of this."

Indy leveled an unflinching glare at me, straight in the eyes. Like she could see through me. Aster was a spectacle of sex, but Indy was the slow burn. Her brown hair flowed over her shoulder, mixing with Aster's blonde. Her high heels were impractical but gorgeous. Her tight body had just enough softness that I had to make a fist. This was my kind of woman, and I didn't know I had a type until I saw her.

The intelligence in her eyes made me want to find out more.

How she could be calm with a gun in the vehicle pointed at her was making me hard.

Zinny was straight-up pissed. She'd already been angry with Aster, but now, being kidnapped, made her a pot of simmering acid. She was the embodiment of a disturbed wasp nest. Red hair and skin littered with flattering freckles. These women that we took in place of who we were really looking for were more than placeholders.

This was my mission. This was my fuck-up. I wish I could say my intel on the Lady Mafia was sturdy, but they were chameleon ghosts in the mist. Everyone was taking guesses, and these ladies were mine. Most importantly, I needed to be in the building where it was all going down.

In my ear, I heard Falcon say, "We've got nothing. No one else that could possibly be them on that plane."

"Let's proceed. We'll hash it out when we get there."

"Now, he's talking to himself! He's insane. He hears voices, for crap's sake. I wanted to make it to thirty. I mean, don't I deserve that?" Aster flopped on her back, her ginormous boobs settling on her chest like two huge Jell-O molds upended on a tabletop.

Zinny folded her arms in front of her. "He's got on an earpiece. I think they screwed up."

"All before my wedding." Aster struggled to sit up, and Indy pushed on her back to help her. Aster pointed a well-manicured finger at me.

"Do you know how many hours it takes to plan a wedding? How many decisions need to be made? This is a monumental event. And now I won't be there. I'll be dead. They'll have to have my wedding without me. And that is so goddamn sad." She flounced backward, her breasts sloshing around like overfull cups of water on a rocking boat.

I rubbed my forehead, trying to think. I had Falcon in my ear telling me I was a jackass. The girls in this car were yelling at me, and I was pretty sure Lev had just run a red light.

Saving my brother was going down the toilet fast, and I was probably three times more likely to die over the whole situation than Aster thought she was.

"Lev, drive normal. Falcon, we need three girls. We've got three girls. We move forward as is." I pointed the gun at the women. "And hush, all of you. And you, stop looking at me like I kicked your puppy." I pointed at Indy with the pinkie on my left hand.

We'd get to the hotel in a few minutes. I'd separate everyone and go over my intel. I had to salvage something out of this giant shovelful of crap I'd just served myself.

FOUR

H ot Suit wanted peace and quiet. He had no idea that when Aster was suffering from an allergic reaction combined with alcohol, she wasn't going to be quiet about anything.

"Did you know Spenser is so sweet? He tells me I'm the most beautiful woman that he's ever seen in his whole life." She touched her engagement ring.

Zinny snorted. Oh no. Zinny on alcohol was the realest person. She was honest, brutally honest.

"As long as you damn near kill yourself to blow your tits up, that is." She kept looking out the window.

"You know, Z, I think you're jealous. Yup, I'm saying it. Where's your man? You got one? You got a ring on your finger?" Aster held up her hand and let the diamond sparkle.

I watched Hot Suit. He was shifting in his seat and appeared super uncomfortable. He met my eyes again and slowly shook his head like he was answering his own question.

"That's shitty of you and you know it." Zinny tipped her head so she was looking in her lap.

Zinny was dealing with a rough breakup. Both she and her man still loved each other, but they couldn't be together anymore.

"I'm sorry. That was a low blow." Aster sniffled twice before nodding then kneading her breasts. "I'm getting to the tingle stage."

"Shit." Zinny threw her hands in the air.

"Why is that bad?" Leto asked. "I need to know whatever's next for this shit show."

"The tingles give her spontaneous orgasms. It's a side effect of the shrimp comedown." I shrugged.

LETO

The moaning and writhing that Aster exhibited would stop a train. She was so dramatic and pornographic. After Aster's first blisteringly effective orgasm, the tears that had waited until her orgasm was over crested quickly.

Aster continued as if all the guys listening weren't turned on. "Z, let's not fight. It's my bachelorette party."

I held up my index finger and interrupted, "Technically, it's a kidnapping."

Zinny ignored me and flipped off Aster. "Okay, but telling me I'm jealous? Saying I need a man?"

Aster interrupted with another screaming, panting orgasm like she was screwing a ghost.

Lev pulled over and watched in the rearview mirror as Aster put on the show. She went for fifteen minutes straight. The other men opened the doors and stood around watching.

When she finally collapsed, Falcon lit a cigarette, inhaled, and exhaled a smoke ring. "Alright, let's pack up these blue balls and get where we're heading."

He passed the smoke to Lev who took a puff as well. We all felt like we needed a hit after Aster's performance.

Falcon stepped forward, put his hands under Aster's armpits, and hoisted her up and out of the car. "I'll take this one. Traveling with them all in the same car seems like a bad idea."

I didn't like Falcon making decisions for the group. This was my job. The payoff happened for having all three of the women together. Obviously, the right women, but that was a concern for later.

After stepping closer to Indy, I signaled to the guys that we'd do as Falcon recommended.

Zinny pushed her way closer to Aster. "She doesn't go alone with you. She's compromised."

Aster flung her arm around Falcon, her giant boob bouncing off his chin. Then her knees went weak as she had another all-out orgasm while screaming in Falcon's face. He supported her lower back as she had the body rippling extravaganza again. By the time she was done, they were both panting.

"Sweet Lord, you come pretty." Falcon held out his hand to Lev for his smoke and took another suck. "I'm gonna need something a lot stronger than this to hang around this chick."

Lev threw the keys after I held up my hand. "I'll meet you at Topic. The penthouse is for us. Use the back entrance and the private elevator. Don't let anyone see these ladies."

After Indy was steered to the passenger side, she watched her friends get into a car together. The less these girls fought, the better. I started the car, and when I put it in drive, she turned to me.

"They better be safe."

Her tone made me look at her harder. She spoke with more steel than I was expecting. "My guys listen to me. They'll be fine."

She met my eyes for a few more beats and then we both looked away.

FIVE

"What's your name?" I rolled down the window a bit, letting the wind whistle through the gap, setting my hair flying around.

"They call me Leto." He checked the rearview mirror

"Who's they?" No phone, but I still had my purse. I wanted information. I was pretty much sober, which at 11 A.M. on the day of my kidnapping, I was grateful for. I may have a headache soon, but that was probably the least of my issues.

He leaned forward, adjusting the seat. "Can't tell you that. Not that it'd matter."

"You know what I should be doing? We had a spa appointment for foot rubs. Like, medical grade foot rubs with spiritual music. I love foot rubs. But instead, I watched my friend blow herself up on purpose, and got kidnapped by a hot guy in a suit. I'm pretty sure we can get into the nitty-gritty, Leto." I shifted my hips and shoulders so I was facing him instead of the road.

He eased off the highway onto an exit ramp. "We're almost there."

"Topic? I've never even heard of it."

He had an earpiece in. I could see it now that I was staring into his ear. His jaw was the kind they put in cologne commercials. He also smelled good, which was pissing me off. A guy should not be good-looking when he is kidnapping you.

"That's good. They keep it out of the news." He turned on his left blinker.

"We again. How big is this organization? Just how much trouble are you driving three nice girls from Westchester into?" I put my hand on the dashboard and started tapping my fingernails.

"You know what? You're not even remotely scared enough for this whole situation." He looked over at me and we locked gazes. He gave me chills. The way it felt when our eyes met.

"Maybe you're not scary enough, Leto. Try harder." I tapped my fingernails some more.

He reached over and covered my hand, pressing on it lightly so I couldn't tap anymore. "Don't ask for what you can't handle."

He tipped his chin up and gave me a tough guy look. I lifted my eyebrow and licked my lips. "You'd have to know me better to know what I can handle."

He tsked at me, pulling his hand away. "You like playing with fire?"

"You saw my friends." I shrugged.

"You've got a point." He put on his blinker again, and it struck me as terribly banal to worry about signaling during a kidnapping.

We pulled to a spot behind a dumpster. After Leto escorted me out, the other SUV pulled in behind us. All the men from the car that held Aster and Zinny hopped out at once, covering their crotches.

Leto tossed up his hands. "Don't leave them in there alone!"

Falcon grabbed the door handle and manhandled Zinny out of the car. The parking lot was filled with Aster's blistering orgasm screams.

He slammed the door shut. "She's been like that the whole damn time."

Zinny waved at me. "You okay?"

She was not as sober as I was. I could tell from her slight imbalance on her heels. She grabbed Lev to stay steady.

"I'm going to take her up." Leto was scanning the area, checking out the upper levels of the hotel where people could possibly see us.

I didn't like the idea that I was leaving the girls in the parking lot, but there were few people as bitchy as Zinny in the world when she was drunk and the men had guns, so...

True to his description of his boys before, there was a back door that led directly to an elevator. Leto put his hand on my elbow to steer me in the obvious direction.

After the brushed gold doors sealed us in, the elevator rocketed upward without needing a button pressed.

"How long will she be like that?" He leaned back against the elevator. Crisp jaw, ticking with frustration. This guy was the kind of handsome that had people forget what they were saying.

"The orgasming? Oh, she'll be out of that stage soon." The ceiling of the elevator was black marble with little LED lights twinkling inside them.

"There's no way out, if that's what you're looking for." His face was set in what had to be his tough guy look. I bet he practiced it from time to time.

"Thanks, Leto. That's awesome. I can't believe I mistook you for a hero back at the airport." I shifted my weight from one hip to the other and he watched the motion.

He sucked on his teeth. "Well, I can't believe I thought you were a member of an elite assassin group."

"I guess we're both disappointments then." I lifted an eyebrow and gave him a look that I hoped conveyed my feelings.

The doors slid open to a stunning view of Slots, Maryland. The neon lights and glittering hotels that we had managed to avoid seeing now rose up in the distance.

"Nice place." I walked in. "Is this where you're planning on killing us?"

CHAPTER
SIX

S he was direct, I'd give her that. And hot as hell. She should've been a sniveling pile of flustered begging. Instead, she was more like a disapproving girlfriend.

Alone in this huge penthouse, I let my mind wander to the many beds. She would be tight as a guitar string. The kind of woman that took care of herself every damn day so that every night was a gift.

I needed a drink, and I needed to think. I had to make a mountain out of this tiny molehill I had. I'd been hoping they were the Lady Mafia, and now I had to make them look deadly for a long enough time so that I could save my brother.

I needed three women killers. Instead, I had three women that might just be the death of me.

The Lady Mafia were supposed to be in Slots. This was the culmination of two years of research from all different factions. They were hard to find and then impossible to track. I'd found the hashtag #LadyMaafia on a whim and convinced myself that the pretty ladies attached to the social media posts were hiding in plain sight. That I was the most clever for finding them. Especially when they posted about coming to Slots in the right time frame. But then this complete debacle proved me so, so wrong. So many other guys were out looking for the Lady Mafia as well. Maybe I was blinded by my extraordinary concern for my brother. I had to be in this building, this debacle, to have a chance at saving him. I missed how obviously incorrect these girls were.

I went to the bar and poured myself a gin and tonic. It was too damn early to be drinking, as the women had proved. Indy clicked around on the marble, taking in the furnishings and decorations.

This was the functioning headquarters for Max as he camped at Slots. The Lady Mafia was due to meet up with the Feybis and run a deal. We heard it involved moving four billion dollars. There was a rumor that government agencies were watching for them, too.

Indy leaned over to look at the fish in the giant tank embedded into the wall. There was a price on the Lady Mafia's heads. If someone found the Lady Mafia, they were to bring them to the casino tonight. The security cameras were to be used to scan the faces of the ladies, combining the few blurry images they had with the fingerprints that they'd told us they needed. When Falcon was assigned to my crew, I was suspicious. He was a more senior guy in the organization, and he seemed pissed to have to take orders from me.

Ultimately, I needed to complete this weird mission to save my brother. He was always taking the fall for me when we were kids and taking the punishments I'd earned. As we got older, it seemed that we switched roles. This time would be much worse. I was going to change. I was going to do things differently.

Needless to say, I had a lot riding on this going right and everything to lose when it all came crashing in on my head. And it was about to do just that unless I could get these ladies taken seriously long enough to get to Matt. My intel that he was at the casino somewhere was valid.

The elevator doors tolled a small bell and the rest of the crew and the two girls crowded the living room.

Aster's face was red and her chest was heaving as if she had run three marathons in a row. The orgasms must have taken the piss out of her. She was still swollen in all the right places.

Zinny was holding her up.

Indy crossed the room to help Aster as well. "Do we have a place where she can lie down?"

I pointed to the hallway, and Falcon escorted the women down to the bedrooms.

I called Lev over. "How'd it go?"

Lev's neck was red from the stress of escorting Aster. "Loud."

"Well, you lived." I clicked my tongue.

"Yeah. Will you?" He backed up and folded his arms. Now would be the questions. The mutiny—possibly.

"I can make it work. I just need to have this drink and some quiet." I really needed just that, and I was sure I wasn't going to get it.

The women were back. Instead of lying down, Aster was flinging her arms around again, revived with her anger seemingly at Zinny. "I'm outta here."

"You can't go anywhere. You're kidnapped." I pointed to my gun for emphasis.

Aster stood like Bambi and Zinny held her steady around her waist. "No. We reject your kidnapping. We're partying. Go do your weird mafia bullshit somewhere else." She topped it off with a middle finger.

Falcon ran his hands through his hair. "This is the craziest damn heist in the world. It's a reflection on you, Leto. You need to take this situation by the balls."

He was right, and I hated that he was. This was not how a guy lifted his position in the organization. Even if I could salvage this, the guys could talk about how it went sideways and haywire at the same time.

I pointed at Zinny and Aster with my index finger and pinkie. "Go get them showered up so they can get fancy. I'm taking this one to pick out the outfits."

It was a direction. I wasn't sure if it was a good one, but the guys seemed excited to be involved in showering the girls.

I put my gun in its holster. Indy whispered something to the other girls and then turned her attention to me.

"Their safety and modesty are on you." She narrowed her eyes.

Why I wanted to keep her happy, I wasn't sure. "Nobody better peek at the tits unless they're asked to do so."

A round of disappointed groans emitted from them.

Indy tipped her head, acknowledging that I respected her wishes. "So where are the clothes?"

I was going to take her into a bedroom, and I was sure that was fine. And I was also sure I wouldn't imagine how many different ways I could bend her over.

CHAPTER
SEVEN

Indy

Hot Suit was a conundrum. It was like he was a good guy trapped in a bad guy's job. His eyelashes were distractingly long. I could tell he was pissed, and it made me want to press him more just to see how hot he was when he was angry. But I was old enough to know better. Just because he was good-looking didn't mean he was worth a damn.

Aster and Zinny being happy with each other made my heart lighter. Spenser had gotten between them lately and it was sad. It was part of the reason this trip was so important. End of an era.

Leto motioned for me to head to the other end of the penthouse. I opened the double doors as he tilted his head toward.

This must be a premier suite. It was the size of three good hotel rooms smashed together and the walls were made up of more windows than they were drywall.

"There are a bunch of choices in the closet. We need three formal, slinky dresses for each of you. Try to look deadly."

I went to the closet and opened it. It was set up like a store with dresses sorted by colors. I started flipping through them.

"You just always have dresses ready up here?" I pulled a nude colored silk, backless with a slit up the leg. It was my size, and the color would go well with my hair.

"We were expecting women." He sat on the bed and watched me. His suit jacket was unbuttoned. He was shameless in his assessment. I decided to unhinge him with a little show.

I slid my party-in-Slots clothes off and stood in just my bra and thong. I side-eyed him, watching as he shifted around on the bed. Bullseye.

"That's a nice tattoo."

I had an entire back piece of a cherry tree in full bloom, and there was even a branch that crawled down my thigh. I ignored his compliment.

I slid the dress over my head and checked it out in the full-length mirror. I found pumps in my size and slid my heels off and tried on the new ones with the red bottoms. I turned to see how the dress looked in the back.

I heard him inhale roughly. It was time to make him really think about the cleverness of having me here. I purposely swung my hips from side to side and then turned, asking him to zip me up.

The zipper closure started below my hip and followed the shape of my side. Leto made a point to not let his skin touch mine, even when I pressed toward him a bit.

"You're friendly for a kidnap victim," he mumbled.

I felt his breath on my cheek.

"You're not as deadly as a kidnapper should be," I tossed back at him.

He stood then, his suit jacket skimming my bare back. "Don't judge my deadliness by how alive you are."

I burst out laughing. Like quiet, snort-gasping laughter. I took peeks at his face and he went from furious to annoyed to trying not to laugh himself. I sat down on the bed and tried to catch my breath.

"You're shit for a man's ego." He shook his head.

"That means I'm doing my job to piss you off then." I patted his chest.

I looked up to see Zinny and Aster in towels, three men trailing behind them.

"Everything okay?"

Zinny nodded. "They behaved themselves."

Aster in a towel was somehow sexier than nudity. She was obscene. I couldn't say I didn't understand the temptation to eat shrimp and be a vixen, but it couldn't be good for her to play with her body's reactions long-term.

"That outfit's incredible." Aster flopped into the armchair next to Leto.

"I've got some picked out for you guys, too. Check out the closet."

The girls giggled as they closed the door.

Falcon shook his head. "This isn't a slumber party, for crap's sake."

It seemed like Leto and Falcon were about to go at it, so I pointed to the bathroom and slipped past them. It was time to take a travel dirt reducing shower. I went as quickly as I could. He had shampoo and conditioner, so I used that as well. I heard music come on and knew that Aster was still feeling the effects of the shrimp. She loved to dance when the orgasms settled down.

After I was dressed, I cracked the door so I could hear my girls. I spied Falcon sitting on the bed, slack-jawed. Aster was less swollen, but she knew how to work it. Zinny was a great complement to Aster, and she had a mini bottle of wine in her hand.

Leto was in the corner, frowning into his phone. I wasn't under any illusions that this was an actual party. Something was going down, but I wanted to keep the atmosphere as light as I could, letting my girls be themselves and set the tone. I had to watch Leto, though. He seemed slightly panicky, slightly desperate. And desperate people did desperate things.

I opened a few drawers and found a lovely sampling of makeup. I went through my routine as best I could and substituted one product for another where necessary.

After I slicked on the miniature gloss, I checked the mirror to see Leto over my left shoulder. "Nice work."

"Thanks. It doesn't take that much. You want in?" I held up the gloss.

"Nah, I'm good. Listen, I think we need to coordinate. I need you ladies to help me out." He backed up and let me spin toward him.

I looked him up and down. "Are you going to change? 'Cause you all look the same."

"That's the plan. We have to look like everyone else. It's you girls that need to look the part." He tilted his head from one side to the other. "And I think you've managed that."

"I match the imaginary Lady Mafia member you have a picture of in your head?" I tapped the gloss against my palm.

"You're the best we've got." He rocked back on his heels. "And I need a leader to stand with me here. And I think that's you."

"Is that because I'm the only one not twerking right now?" I pointed to the doorway and it framed Aster and Zinny's butts mashing against each other in time to the music.

"That's part of it," he agreed.

"Yeah, the problem is, we're literally abducted. And we don't work for you. And we're not getting a cut of whatever's in this for you. We're just three ladies trying to have some fun on the weekend. The minute you put us in public, I'm screaming like a loon." I put the gloss behind my back and let it fall onto the countertop.

Leto looked to the ceiling. "I'm so fucked."

Maybe it was the desperation in the way he said *fucked*. Maybe it was the fact that my girls were safe and having a good time despite Aster's shrimping. I took the bait.

"Why? Tell me what's fucking you, kidnapper?" I leaned back and crossed my arms over my boobs.

"You wouldn't understand." He angrily jabbed his finger at his phone.

"I hope I can't, because you stuffed us all into a fake Uber and took us here. But, tell me what's going on. What other choice do you have?" A slower song came on and Aster and Zinny started slow dancing with each other. Falcon looked like he might die of happiness.

"I worked for the government for a few years. Then I helped my brother with his business, but he did a few stupid things and now he's in trouble—captured. But if I get this score, get the Lady Mafia, then I can save him. And he can get his business back and get back to business."

I knew my eyebrows were furrowed. "That sounds like a really stupid, convoluted plan."

"See?" He jammed his phone into his pocket and threw his hands in the air. "This is why I didn't want to say anything."

"Won't they realize we're not the Lady Mafia and kill all of us? You included?" I mean, seriously. Anyone could see how that would play out.

"Well, I felt like we could cover your mouths or threaten you some more. That you wouldn't tell them you weren't the Lady Mafia until I was out of the building with my brother. Also, there are so many people here that it will be impossible to kill them all without causing a huge, huge event. Safety in numbers." He rocked from his heels to his toes.

Zinny pulled Aster into the bathroom, which was very spacious, luckily. "What's going on in here? Oh, Indy, that lip color is glorious on you."

Falcon leaned one arm against the doorframe. "You heard from him, right?"

Leto jutted his chin out as an affirmative. "They want the girls there in fifteen or less."

"Where do they want us? Or is this about different girls?" I pushed off the countertop. They'd separated us ladies earlier, and I didn't want it to happen again.

"It's you. Here's the rule. You stay with your man. You do what you're told. If one of you acts up or mouths off?" Leto stepped into my space. "Then the other disappears. Only speak up if you can deal with the guilt of that decision."

I reached a hand out to Zinny, and we squeezed. She did the same to Aster so we were all connected for a moment. And then we were separated.

EIGHT

All I knew was that Max had requested all Lady Mafia suspects to report to the casino's ballroom in Topic.

We were to get each female's fingerprints and make sure that the security cameras viewed them. And what Max asked for, he got. Falcon took Zinny and Switch was on Aster. I had Indy.

I made sure they were a good car length apart, and we each took turns catching the elevator.

When Indy and I stepped in, she prodded me for more information. "So this is like a giant pageant? Where you and all different guys are bringing in who you think might be the Lady Mafia?"

"Sort of like a human lotto ticket. I was sure I was onto something with you three. I followed that hashtag #LadyMaafia." Her ass was literally the shape of a peach. I was dying.

Indy covered her mouth to try to hide her smile. "We've used that hashtag since middle school. Seriously, not a great clue. Weren't you a little concerned when you saw how it was spelled?"

"Whatever." This was going to be horrible. I mean, they looked the part at least, but Max was notorious for throwing out really tough challenges at his people. Rumor was, he was crazy.

Rumor also was, the Lady Mafia were about to make him the richest man on the planet.

I needed just a minor part of those rumors to be true. When the elevator opened to the casino's ballroom, they looked even better. The call for the Lady Mafia had turned up some real desperate people.

There were tons of groups of three. Some looked scared, but most looked clueless. Indy sputtered next to me, "Wow, that's a lot of ladies."

Mobster-looking handlers trailed a group of gray-haired women in bedazzled shirts, each with a huge cup of coins for the slots. There were sorority sisters. There was a group of frazzled looking soccer moms.

Behind me, the elevator closed and then the one next to it opened. Parker, my nemesis, stepped out with three of the dead-liest women I'd ever seen. Each had on black leather with knives and guns strapped to them. All had deep red lips and sharp red nails. One held up her hand in a finger gun and then licked the full length while locking her eyes with me.

"Of fucking course. Goddamn Parker." I put my hand on Indy's lower back, covering part of her tattoo.

"Oh, he found them, alright," she agreed with my disappointing assessment that I hadn't fully verbalized.

"Well, better cut your losses and get out, huh?" Indy's pace quickened. She was headed toward Switch and Falcon who were assessing the new girls with shaking heads. Aster and Zinny were holding hands when they were supposed to be separate.

"Leto, you giant fartbag. Figured you'd show up here and try to save your brother. You know my cousin works for Max, too. Damn shame your brother sucks at taking a beating. But my cousin keeps trying him to toughen him up. Doing the best we can to help out." Parker gave me a huge, cheesy grin.

And that's when my anger took over. I rolled my head on my neck and took my suit jacket off. As I stepped toward him, he moved behind one of his badass ladies. I narrowed my eyes. Lady

Mafia, from their reputation, would be experts in hand-to-hand combat. I swung my arm, fully prepared to stop the punch if she didn't, but instead, she ducked and whimpered.

I felt resistance on my arm and saw Indy holding my elbow. "Don't hit girls, asshole."

I nodded briskly once. She wouldn't know that I wasn't actually planning on making contact.

Zinny and Aster started dancing again, blatantly ignoring the mismatched crowd around them.

Parker helped his one member of the Lady Mafia up off the floor where she was crouched and harshly spoke in her ear.

The music was louder, possibly because of the show Zinny and Aster were putting on. Other women came closer to them and started in as well. The older women, the sorority girls, even the soccer moms.

It was a nice way to sort out the fearful from the ladies that did not know about the real reason they were here.

Indy snagged a glass off the tray of a wandering waiter. It looked like sparkling water. She winked at him and took a sip, getting a bit of her lipstick on the straw.

Indy wrapped her hand around the glass, and I had a good idea. If I could have all the girls take a drink, I was pretty sure Switch could lift their prints off of the glasses. Or better yet...

I signaled to Switch, who took his time walking over to me, grinding against some of the willing ladies. He was the best we had at computers and anything hackable.

I leaned into him. "Do you think you could get a copy of the prints we are looking for? Then we could submit them as these girls' prints?"

I watched as he ran through the options in his head, his facial expressions revealing the likelihood of the ones he considered. Finally, he offered, "I could certainly try. I mean, they have to have them here. I'll need more than my phone, though."

Indy smiled at us. Shit, she was gorgeous. "Go ahead, I'll stay here." She lifted her glass to us in a mock toast.

"Take Falcon as backup. Don't get caught." After turning my back on them, I tried to take her glass from her.

"I'm not done. Mind your business." She took another defiant gulp before observing the group of dancers and shady characters that filled the giant room. "So no one knows who they are, huh?"

"Nope. They've got so many urban legends racked up in the last two years, it's really not possible. My theory," I walked over to an open standing table and she came with me while we conversed, "is that it's a group of dudes that hire different women to take the fall. There's a fairly new group that's risen to the top in the last few years. The guy is covered in a skeleton tattoo, and his buddy —well, they aren't doing stuff like families used to. I think it's them."

"How are your gut impulses, by the way?" She pointed her thumb at herself and swallowed a smile.

"Other than you, pretty good." I grabbed a beer off a different waiter's tray.

"Really. Because whatever choice you made to get yourself in this business seems less than stellar." She set down her glass.

A group of ladies in volleyball jerseys hurried past us with cups full of coins for the slots.

"But other than that, I've got good judgment." The beer was ice-cold and made my entire throat happy. I needed this to calm my nerves and to stay ahead of all the guys in this room. I was used to needing to stay calm, but this was different. Here there were some really familiar faces. Everyone was shooting their load on this payday. I had to say, Parker's girls ticked every box. One kept twirling a knife on her index finger like a professional killer. I'd have to get the deal I had in mind to Max first, before he ever laid eyes on Parker's girls.

Indy finished her sparkling water and tossed the glass onto the floor. "Mazel tov!"

Then she crushed the pieces of glass under her shoes.

"Why the hell did you do that?" I wanted at least the guise of grabbing up her prints.

"Time to dance with my girls. If this is the only time we get to party for Aster, I'm taking it." She threaded through the crowd so quickly, I had to abandon my beer to keep up.

When we got there, I noticed how many men were ogling Aster. Her swelling had decreased slightly, but she was still every bit a pornographic Barbie. And when she wiggled, everything jiggled. Zinny spanked her big booty, and the resulting image was being tattooed in every man's brain in the area.

The music got even louder. It was just barely past lunchtime, but in the club atmosphere, the party the girls were throwing for themselves seemed like it was happening at midnight.

I felt Max's stare on the back of my neck before anyone told me he was here. I swung to confirm what I already knew. One of the most powerful men on the criminal scene had moseyed into the ballroom casino, impeccably dressed in a suit that must have cost more than most cars.

When we made eye contact, his smile slid to the side. I gestured to the three women in front of me. He inspected them from a distance. His eyes went wide briefly at Aster but set to a simmer when he saw Indy.

I looked at Indy, and it was like I could see the electricity crackling between them. It was a high voltage eye fucking.

Damn it all to hell.

There was something about a man in power. A confident air surrounded them like an aura. Most men would look around the room, but the guy I was currently locked in a staring battle with hadn't done that at all. He knew what he was looking for. The people in the rest of the space were familiar with what to expect. He was a heat-seeking missile for trouble, and now he was laser-focused on me.

I broke eye contact and focused on Zinny and Aster, moving with them while they danced. I could feel the attention of the new guy and Leto. Things were happening around us. Lots of movement. I peeked over my shoulder to see, and yup, Laser Focus was headed right at me and his security—who were not wearing suits like everyone else, but black turtlenecks and black pants—seemed to swarm the edges of the room.

I felt Leto touch my back again. "Listen. Stay cool, okay?"

And that was my cue to not stay cool, but to look for an escape. Whatever was going down in this room would not end well. There were far too many guns and far too many hotheaded-looking guys.

The ladies had their hands on each other's shoulders, but they looked angry. Fighty. I caught Zinny's eye and gave her a wink.

Zinny pried Aster's fingers off of her shoulders one digit at a time. "What? It's true. I can't watch you marry him and not say something."

The scream that Aster emanated was a gut-wrenching mix of pain and anger. The men all around the room pulled their weapons out.

"You *what*?" Aster staggered backward, and I put out a hand to stop her from falling.

"I slept with Spenser last week." Zinny's words ground the music to a halt. Everyone was frozen. Laser Focus Sex Eyes Leto. Everyone.

"My fiancé?!" Aster held out her ring again. "You're that desperate?"

I watched as the remorse slid from Zinny's face. "I screwed him, and I barely felt it."

"Bitch!" and "Husband stealer!" reverberated through the room.

Zinny had a hothead when she was angry. "I'm shocked that you don't blow up after sucking on his shrimp dick, because it's small and it makes my skin crawl." Zinny pushed forward.

Everyone was gathering around as the ladies started a proper fight.

I never imagined the giant ball of tumbling fighting existed outside of cartoons, but it did. Right there on the dance floor. Aster's whole ass was hanging out of the back of her tube sock dress, and Zinny was wearing very extensive Spanx.

I bobbed and weaved, adjusting the ladies' outfits in between blows.

"Of all the dicks in the world you could ride? Why? Why would you pick Spenser? You hate me that much?" Aster was fighting way dirtier than Zinny. Zinny seemed angry, but also aware that Aster was more impaired than she was. Twice I watched Zinny prevent Aster from face-planting.

"It's always about him. Spenser this and Spenser that. What happened to chick flick night? Dildo shopping? Who's going to go to Broadway with me?" Zinny pulled on Aster's hair. Aster tried to slap Zinny in the face. I was resigned that the fight was going to play out to the bitter end, and there was only so much I could do to prevent the nudity. Aster's lady humps were real migrators.

"You're only worrying about you? You know I wanted this. And now you took it all away. No princess day for me." Realizing this deflated Aster and she sat on the floor, looking forlorn. "Maybe I'll marry him anyway. Maybe we just won't talk about it."

Zinny threaded her fingers behind her neck. "Man, dude. Man. You can't do it. I mean, he wasn't even sorry."

Aster wiped at her eyes with the back of her hands and quietly added, "This was supposed to be *my* big day."

The crowd was hemming and hawing. A few guys were putting bets together. This was an issue. A huge issue. None of these people understood that the three of us were like sisters. We were soulmates.

Of course, we fought, but we could always trust each other, and we always had each other's backs.

"Enough," Laser Focus Sex Eyes basically murmured, but everyone listened.

I grabbed both Aster and Zinny by the upper arms.

"Whose girls are these?" he asked, still calm, still quiet, while narrowing his eyes.

I snuck a glimpse at Leto. It seemed like he was deciding whether to claim us when Parker cleared his throat.

"Leto, sir. We ran into them by the elevators. He sure took all your warnings to heart. Obviously." Parker gave Leto a smarmy smile and a wink.

Max looked over the crowd before leaning close to one of his guards. In the next minute, Leto was being escorted deeper into the casino.

CHAPTER
TEN

W ell, this was it. I was going down in flames. Everything else was fucked. Max led me into a theater room with plush deep velvet red seats. He picked a row and then chose a seat, gesturing to the choices next to him.

I took the cue and picked a seat away from him. The man distance away from him. I mean, I thought that was the right call. Room to spread our legs for our manhood. Oh sweet Jesus. I'm going to die thinking about another man's manspread and what a stupid way to go. I tried to picture Indy in her underwear quickly.

The clicking I heard made me realize how scary movie theaters were. The space behind me seemed endless. Was it a gun? I had to get through my panic to realize that Max was messing with a ballpoint pen.

He addressed me, "Feel guilty about something? You're jumpy."

"In my defense, this is one hell of a party, and I need to perform well to save my brother." I shifted, and the chair squeaked. An old theater. The chairs weren't tall or recliners like any of the new places had. Things that didn't matter. I had to figure my way out of this for Matt.

"Good point. So, do you want to tell me why the girls you brought are making a spectacle of themselves out there?" He grabbed the armrest, and a spider tattoo on his hand flexed with the tendons.

You wouldn't know how deadly Max was from just a picture of him—if he hid his spider tattoo, that was. In person, there was no denying it. Maybe evil. Maybe ending so many timelines early. Maybe getting to the top and doing what he had to do to stay there.

"Hey, they were supposed to be going to a bachelorette party. They're having a lot of emotions." Which made little sense for seasoned assassins and I knew that. I had to think quickly, do stuff that made a difference with how this was going to play out. "But Indy said she had info on the Lady Mafia, so I brought her. Because no one you have out there right now is the real deal."

I was taking a chance. Bluffing. These were the things in my comfort zone.

"Is that so? Fine. Get her in here." He launched the direction over his shoulder. "Which one is that? The overblown sex robot, the redhead, or my future wife?"

I knew my eyes were bugging out of my head as I whipped my head around on my shoulders. "What? You know Indy already?"

Max shrugged and managed a hint of a smile. "Nope. I can just tell."

INDY

The casino was tense and each set of kidnappers and kidnappees were lumped together. The music was off. Falcon had taken the lead the second Leto disappeared.

"Listen, we gotta get outta here. They're gonna kill us in the

Return or replace your item
Visit Amazon.com/returns

1959285041 9781959285045
1959285041
Anastasia, Debra --- Paperback
Lady Mafia   1

Qty. Item

Order of April 6, 2023

SdqfVCyVnz

amazon.com

A gift for you

Enjoy your gift! Congratulations on winning!! From kreadssmut

amazon Gift Receipt

Send a Thank You Note

You can learn more about your gift or start a return here too.

Scan using the Amazon app or visit
https://a.co/d/f3KJM8U

Lady Mafia

dicks. A lot." Falcon stepped forward and draped an arm around Aster. "This orgasm pinata is my party favor."

Switch pointed at Zinny. "I like a challenge. This one is mine."

"Maybe go in different directions. Just a suggestion." I could see the other three trying to decide if they should take me. I helped them along. "You know, you'll move quicker without me."

And then the door popped open. One of Max's men came right for me.

Then my crew of people were gone. I stood still because there was no point in running. The man that came for me gave the rest of the room a hard glare. He didn't have to touch me. I just walked toward him. Inevitably, I was going in.

I made my way through the hallways lined with his men and a few women, all in the same outfit. When I was directed to a theater, I vaguely wondered why I didn't smell popcorn before I shook myself back to the moment.

Both Max and Leto turned in their seats, expecting me, clearly. Instead of sitting down between them, I went to the row in front and leaned against the back of the seat. "Gentlemen?"

Leto looked sketchy and worried. Max looked like he was ready to film a music video, in control and pretty proud of himself.

Leto sat up straighter and tried to fill me in until Max held up one finger. "Nope. You said she knows, so I want to hear it from her."

It was a trap. Leto had said I knew something, but I had to guess what the hell it was.

"I know a lot of things. I can tell you how long it takes an avocado to ripen. I can give you the life cycle of a kangaroo." And then I looked at Max's face. The eye contact made my ovaries kick. He knew how to look at a woman. I had to glance at the wall to take a break from his intense gaze.

Movement in my peripheral vision forced me to look back at Max. He'd stood. He was tall, intimidating. He moved in front of

Leto and skirted the other seats until he was in my row. Max put his foot on the side of my heels. I watched as our feet almost touched.

I lifted my head to face whatever he was going to deal out to me. This crazy, dangerous guy.

"You've got something for me, Indy?"

My name on his mouth made me inhale quickly and exhale in a whistle. "Depends on what you want."

My answer sounded more sexual than I meant it to. My nipples were perma-hard, being this close to him. My goddamn vagina was a fickle bitch and a traitor. She liked danger. She liked risk. I needed her to take up skydiving or something so I could get through this whole debacle alive.

He leaned down, close to my ear, not touching me, but the heat of his breath let me know he could. Because he was just an infinitesimal movement away from being flush against my body. "I want a buffet of everything I can't see of yours right now. And a few things I can." He moved closer, his lips brushing the shell of my ear. "But first..." He took two deep breaths. I watched his chest rise and fall correspondingly. He touched his tongue to his lips before putting his index finger over them. I focused on the intricate spider tattoo on his hand. "Everyone's here for a reason, and I think you know what it is."

"They like gambling?" I didn't pull away, or lean back. I didn't really want to give him space.

"You certainly do if you're not being honest with me." His breath was on my cheek now. I could see his half-closed eyes as I heard him sniff my hair.

"So you want to know what I know about Lady Mafia?" I watched Leto's eyes twitch with surprise. Either I had guessed right or very, very wrong.

Max's low laughter played over my clit like a drum. "The lady is all in."

"Usually." I turned my head so my lips and his were almost touching.

Maybe I was imagining it, but all the men in the theater room seemed to lean toward me, edgy for more information.

Max held his hand out to me, palm up. "Shall we go figure out what you know?"

I didn't give him my hand. "Honestly, first, I want to know what's happened to Leto's brother. Then we'll talk."

Max closed his eyes. "Really? Do you think I tip my hand that easily?"

"Your hopes rest on a lady that was accidentally kidnapped from the airport. I'm guessing your cards are crap." The tension between us crackled.

He took the back of his hand and let it run from my shoulder to my elbow. "Careful. You're talking far too much."

What did I have to lose in the situation? We were all toast. I pushed off from the seat and snapped my teeth at him.

His laughter began again. Straight under my dress was where it landed. He snatched my wrist and spun me, putting his arm across my hips. "Let's go talk," he said into the nape of my neck. Chills again.

Now, I was speaking to a dark movie theater screen. "You can take me, but if you want cooperation, I need to see Leto's brother."

"Are you two a thing? You and Leto?" Max still hadn't been rough with me, just forceful.

"Not yet." I baited him a little. Not afraid to use the dudes against each other. As far as I knew, Aster and Z were out of the building with Falcon and Switch. Hopefully, they had made it all the way out.

But that was another concern for later. First things first. "Where's Matt?"

Max shook his head while turning me around. "Okay. I'll play along. Darco, get me a picture of the brother."

I rolled my eyes. "I don't want a picture you could have taken days ago. Bring him here."

"So all of a sudden you know how to negotiate for hostages?" The skeptical look clouded his handsome face.

"Only if the man that has them has a crush on me." I was leaning a bit into the sexpot thing, which might have consequences I wasn't ready for.

"Darco, bring Matt up on FaceTime." The guard pulled out his phone and sent a few texts before the ringtone for FaceTime filled the theater.

When the camera flashed in my direction, Leto jumped out of his seat and closed the distance. "You okay, bro? You good?"

Matt seemed okay, nodding, but looking to his left quickly every time he went to say a word.

I blurted, "Where are you? Is it here? In the casino?"

I saw Matt nod once before Darco swung the camera away from us and disconnected. I wasn't sure if Leto had seen the beginning of the affirmative motion.

Leto slapped the seat in front of him. "What the fuck is going on?"

Max pushed on Leto's chest, causing him to fall back into his theater seat.

Max met my gaze steadily and then uttered a curt, "Good?" in Leto's direction.

I responded with a slight movement of my head. "That works for me."

Max took my hand and led me from the theater. I peered over at Leto, and he watched me leave with his head held low, his expression clearly dejected.

CHAPTER
ELEVEN

Well, that was a pile of crap. Indy left with Max—somehow bargaining her way into letting me see Matt, which was clever. Pointless, but clever.

Now, I had no pretend Lady Mafia to bargain for my brother's safety. And even worse than that, Matt was already trapped. Maybe even worse than that—if possible—was that my brother now knew I failed and had seen my disappointing face.

Darco came up to me. "Stand, douchebag. You gotta go back out to the casino. No one needs you here."

He slapped me on the back of the head immediately. I was going to abandon Indy now. Max would have the girl I liked and my brother. And I was getting marched out to the most somber casino party I'd ever witnessed. Probably the only party I would ever witness again. The door that led to the theater shut behind me.

I found a discarded tray with a fresh beer, so I snatched it up. I gulped the amber liquid, feeling it quench my parched throat. I needed to think. Be a hero for someone in this situation. I was going down. My brother didn't have to die for his sins, and Indy deserved to finish her weekend in Slots with her girls.

Speaking of which, I looked around the room and couldn't find any of my people.

I patted my pockets, but remembered that Max's men took my phone when I had to go in the back. I had no way of contacting them.

Had they left the property altogether?

It was time to be unpredictable. I ripped my shirt off and pounded my chest. I'd gotten everyone's attention. I hopped up on top of the nearest table, kicking the glasses off. Once I had everyone's attention, I started a riot.

I cupped my hands around my mouth. "Ladies! There is no Lady Mafia. These guys are going to kill everyone here."

I made a grand gesture of pointing to as many women as I could.

There was absolute silence. The different kidnappers held their heads, others drew their guns, and some tried to get their hands on their kidnappees.

A few of Max's men came for me. I hopped off the table and flipped it toward them.

How this was going to help, I didn't know. But chaos felt like the only sane option I had. Or insanity. However you wanted to look at it.

Screams and fighting permeated the air.

I wanted to figure out where my brother was or die trying.

Max was ready for the mutiny. His people had the casino on lockdown with just a few words. He stood by the pit boss for a few minutes while everyone realized they were trapped. Then he started a slow clap that was accompanied by a creepy smile.

"Bravo, Leto. Way to panic everyone. I could have found out what I needed and let a lot of people continue to have their vacation in Slots none the wiser." He stopped clapping and rested his hands on the banister. "Say thank you, everyone!"

No one said anything, but all the glares I was getting pretty much summed up a giant *fuck you* instead.

As I looked around the room, I realized I was stuck. This was a trap. I looked at my hands, thinking of my brother and Indy. Life was coming up to smack me hard in the nuts.

The hushed chaos that existed was a distraction. The black masks on Max's men added to the drama. I knew Max was pissed with me, but clearly not pissed enough to kill me on the spot. I shuffled deeper into the crowd. Some of the women that knew what they were here for seemed like they expected to have their lives threatened. Some were for sure hearing about the fact that they were in danger for the first time. The ladies in the volleyball jerseys couldn't stop sneaking in a crank on the slots from time to time.

I kept my head down and continued to step backward until my back was to a wall. One of the older women in the crowd passed out and I took the moment to squeeze out the exit door that had been blocked by a guard. He'd stepped forward to see what had happened. Curiosity kills the cat and also makes the building less secure.

I padded down the stairs and made my way back down to the vehicles. I guessed that my guys would go there to reconvene or leave me here entirely. They had no loyalty to me.

Sure enough, as I reached the back of the car Falcon had been assigned, I saw that it was packed with people. I tapped on the back glass and the back door flung open.

Curses and harassment from Zinny and Aster about Indy met me. I held up both my hands until I had quiet. Once I did, I saw that the SUV parked next to Falcon was also filled with my guys.

"Indy is still there. Max has taken a liking to her. My brother is also still in there." I held my wrist with one hand and made a fist with the other.

"Wait, hold up. Your brother is in there? He works for Max?" Falcon was on my admission like a lady at a dress sale.

"No, he's a hostage. Just like Indy. I was hoping to get him in the trade for the Lady Mafia." I had to be honest with everyone. They needed to know that this mission was personal for me.

Though I wasn't sure it would change what they thought of me as a person.

Falcon lit a cigarette. Aster took it out of his mouth and pinched the lit end until it was extinguished.

"I have very few working nerve endings in my fingers when I'm coming off the shrimpies." Aster tossed the butt at my feet. "Except in the dick holster. They're popping down there."

Every guy in earshot responded as if they planned it, "We *know*."

Her orgasming trick was really getting on everyone's nerves, clearly. She was less swollen, I noticed. Her dress was baggy in a few key spots.

Zinny leaned forward. "You need to save your brother, so you used this convoluted idea about the Lady Mafia to get to the man that has him?"

She'd summarized all my bad choices, so I nodded that she was correct.

"Damn, you couldn't fart yourself out of a paper bag, could ya?" Falcon started in with a deep laugh.

Zinny squinted at me and snapped her fingers until the guys who had joined in with Falcon settled down. "There's no giant payoff, but you all work for money, right? Aster's fiancé will pay for Indy to be rescued from here."

Aster sniffled. "He would do that, wouldn't he?"

Zinny shrugged her shoulders. "Your party tits and ass are pretty unique. And if he doesn't pay up, I'll blackmail him into doing it by saying I'll tell you I slept with him."

Aster sighed and slumped back. "We can't go home without Indy. No matter what. Even if it costs me Spenser."

In unison, again, my men shouted, "Spenser's a *pussy*!"

Aster wrinkled her nose. She almost whispered, "Y'all don't even know him," but seemed resigned to the fact they were right.

I knew I had to take the deal Zinny was offering before Falcon did. He'd be seen as the leader immediately.

"Show me his Insta. If he's rocking that kind of wealth, he'll flash it." I crossed my arms over my chest like I had a choice. This was the only option.

Aster held out her hand and Falcon put a phone into it. After a few seconds, she handed me the phone.

Spenser certainly did have an Instagram, and it was chock-full of assholery. Only pictures of Aster all blown up from shrimp were featured. None of whatever she looked like deflated. I was thinking Zinny was right. Spenser was a dick. Luxury cars and fancy watches were mixed in with exotic locations.

"Good enough for me." I handed the phone back to Falcon and tried to play it cool. Every second I wasted on this farce was a chance that Max would realize I was gone and kill my brother before I even got a chance to save him.

"We're coming with you. I want to make sure you expend every effort to get Indy, and not just Matt." Zinny pushed her way out of the vehicle and into my corralling arms.

"Well, we need everybody. I've got a plan. Huddle up."

INDY

For a prison, it was lush. I was expecting a loading dock or a basement full of boxes. Instead, after going through three locked doors, as luxurious as the room Leto had taken us to but with the addition of a hot tub.

Matt from the video earlier was in the hot tub, a fresh round of bubbles trapped in his chest hair. In person I could see the resemblance between Leto and his brother.

The guard pushed me into the room and pointed at the snacks on the table. "Eat. Max says he treats people well. Remember that."

I walked over to the table and picked up a piece of mozzarella cheese. "Tell him he's a great warden."

I was holding my heels in my other hand and tossed them near the couch. I looked around. This was a brilliant place for criminals to meet. I walked to a panel of curtains, and when I pushed them aside, I saw only cement. One entrance. No exit. It was smart. A fire trap, but smart for what Max was using it for.

I tested the water in the hot tub with my fingertips. Lovely. I sat on the edge and pulled my feet around, dipping them in. I hissed at the wet heat of it all. It felt amazing. Then I slipped in wearing my fancy dress. Matt raised his eyebrows when he saw my lack of a swimsuit. After sliding under the bubbles, I groaned. I loved how the water hit my muscles.

"Who are you? And what are you going to do to me?" Matt tucked his feet closer to his body.

"I have no plans for you. I'm a prisoner, too, so maybe we have a little in common. What are you in for?" I glanced around. We had two guards at the front of the door.

"I did something stupid, so I'm here as bait. Or the ransom. Wait, you were on the FaceTime. How's my brother? " Matt splashed the water in the hot tub by snapping his fingers.

"I am and I don't know. Have they hurt you?" I rolled my head on my neck. I didn't realize how much tension all the kidnapping was forcing on me.

"Not yet. It's implied. Hence the reason I'm drinking naked in this hot tub." He looked down between his legs. I didn't. It wasn't his fault I slipped into his tub.

"There's just that one door?" I leaned forward a little and my hair drifted on top of the bubbles.

"That's the only one they're coming in and out of." He reached down next to his hips and came back with a glass that was full of hot tub water. "My gin."

"Yeah, it's in here with you now." I spotted the bottle on the floor outside the tub and pushed myself to sit on the edge. I told him to grab my ankle and leaned back to snag it.

After I was sitting back up, Matt praised my abs, then apologized, "I'm sorry. I shouldn't be hitting on a prisoner."

I grabbed his glass and poured it out, before filling it up with more alcohol. He held out his hand expectantly and I smiled as I downed the drink. "I'm not your maid, friend."

I handed him the bottle and the glass so he could fill it up himself. He kept missing the glass and pouring the expensive booze into the tub. I swung my legs out and stood up. My dress was ruined and stuck to me. I flipped my hair as I walked up to one of the guards.

"Can I get an outfit off of you guys? I think I'm going to catch a cold. This air conditioning is super frigid." I covered my nipples with my hands.

The one with the spiky red hair darted his eyes around and then coughed into his hand.

"Please?" I feigned a shiver.

He looked at the other guard who shrugged. The guard wordlessly walked to a bedroom and pointed at a closet. Inside, there were multiple choices of the all black outfits that the guards wore. I picked out the closest to my size that I could find, a black turtleneck and pants with the waist rolled and pinched up. I stuck my feet into a set of combat boots that were too big.

I smiled at the guard who had watched the whole costume change. I gave him a wink and walked around him, murmuring thanks when I was close to his shoulder.

In the hallway I saw another door and pretended to not understand where I needed to go. I got a quick glimpse before the guard caught up to me and pulled the door shut.

There had been an arsenal in there. Granted, a lot of the spaces on the wall were empty—but there were still a lot of guns. The guard put his hand on my shoulder and moved me back to the living room. Matt had gotten out of the hot tub and was sitting in a pair of soggy pants. I pointed to his situation and gave the guard puppy eyes. I heard him sigh and he disappeared into the bedroom and returned with a black outfit for Matt.

Once Matt had switched his wet pants for dry ones and a shirt as well, we both sat on the couch. Our helpful guard manned the door again.

"Did they tell you who they're looking for?" I leaned closer to Matt.

"No, but I heard them talking about the Lady Mafia. I thought it was a new movie or something." He eyed the guards.

"Or something." I scanned the room again. There were a few air vents, so there *were* other ways out besides the door. More complicated, but ways.

TWELVE

O n our way back into the building, we encountered Max's guys. We'd taken out enough of them that each of us had an outfit that resembled the guards, topped off with masks. Also, we had their guns.

We were pretending to guard the women we had kidnapped while we went in to rescue the other woman we'd kidnapped that was now kidnapped by a new kidnapper. I needed another drink to make this whole thing make sense.

Last I knew, Indy was with Max. And I couldn't imagine him doing anything but taking her to bed with the way their gaze sizzled when they looked at each other.

I indicated to the guys that we should head back to the casino. When we muscled our way past the guards, things had changed.

The casino was separated into groups. One was clearly the women that were obviously not the Lady Mafia. The others were possibilities. So my big announcement hadn't dissuaded Max completely.

We marched the girls over to the not possible Lady Mafia and set them down.

Parker was pleading his case for the guards to take him up to

Max to discuss why his girls were the right ones. I tilted my head for the guys to stay with Zinny and Aster as I walked up to Parker.

"Boss wants to talk to him." I pointed at the man with my pinkie.

The guard's eyebrows knitted together. "Really? Max says this one is a clown."

I felt delighted as Parker's face fell before he forced his bluster back up.

"I don't know. I don't ask questions. Do you?" I pushed Parker with the palm of my hand.

I took Parker up to Max's theater wordlessly. He, on the other hand, was full of bargains, lies, and bragging. He promised me girls, money, and cars. After looking in the theater, there was no Max. I grunted. He had to be somewhere else.

I approached another guard. "Where's Max?"

Parker whirled on me but didn't say anything. The other guard pointed down the hallway. "His room."

I nodded like I knew where that was. When we were a few paces away, Parker hissed at me, "You don't know what the hell you're doing?"

I pushed him forward like the question itself was a punch. "Shut up, asshole."

I did have a plan of sorts, so he could shove it. I listened carefully and could hear someone talking on the other side of the farthest door. I knocked once and opened it like I had every right to be there.

Max turned slowly, phone to his ear, and then tilted his head like a confused puppy. I thrust Parker forward again.

"He had something to say, sir."

Max covered the end of the phone with his palm. "About what?"

"His girls." I stepped backward, like delivering Parker was really my official job.

"I asked not to be interrupted." He moved his hand and ran it through his hair.

"Of course. But this guy said he had information." I poked Parker in the shoulder to encourage him to speak up.

"Ugh, yeah. Mr. Max, sir. I have three very convincing women downstairs. They are for sure the Lady Mafia. I think we can call off the search for them because I have them here with me." Parker stepped from one side to the other, bouncing on his toes. He was far from the guy that was swaggering around before.

"Are you saying you think I've had them here under my nose all this time but somehow...missed them? That I've been searching for these girls—for this crew for over a year and I could be that dumb?" Max hung up his phone and slid it into his pocket.

Parker hemmed and hawed, "No. Of course, you would know. I mean, if anyone would know, it'd be you. You're an expert on those ladies, for sure."

I had a passing thought that Parker should run for office. He was a slippery dude.

Parker had seemed to talk himself into a corner. Finally, he got honest instead of ass kissy. "I don't know, man. You've got ladies down there my grandmother's age and I overheard a group of soccer moms talking about the benefits of fiber. I followed the brief. I did the research. My girls are solid." With that said he stepped back a little.

A flurry of emotions painted themselves on Max's chiseled face. "Very well. Take him and bring up his women. We'll put them through their paces."

I pulled on Parker's shoulder, making him head out of the room. I was getting more chaos started, but I very well may have convicted three more girls to their doom in my ass backward way of trying to save Matt.

THIRTEEN

The guards looked like they would rather be anywhere else. They were being lax with Matt and me, letting us talk.

"How long were you expecting they'd keep you?" He seemed distracted.

"I was hoping for the last few days that it would be the next day. Seeing you show up here has diminished the hope considerably."

I pouted my lips in confusion. "What do you mean when I showed up?"

"Well, you seem out of their ordinary routine. Which means something is going to shake up and I'm not sure what." Matt started tapping his toes.

"When we were kids, my brother and I used to play the best games. All we had were a laundry basket and a head full of imagination, but we would get lost in our own worlds for hours. When things were getting boring, we would switch up the game by shouting, 'Shuffle.' And no one questioned it. I can't tell you how many times I wanted to shout, 'Shuffle.' It all feels like a very real game."

He seemed genuine.

"Well, it's real, sunshine. What I need to know is where your loyalty lies? If I can get us a way out, do you want to take it?" Getting to the other part of the basement suite would not be easy, but harder things had been done.

Matt thought for a few seconds. I wondered how much he had been drinking. Eventually, he answered, "As long as it won't get Leto or me in any more trouble. Yeah, I'd go."

I assessed the room. The guards were both looking at their phones. Matt was not giving them reason to be concerned. And me? I was just a lady. Not scary at all.

"Follow my lead." I took off across the room at a leisurely pace. I didn't want the guards catching wind that they were now in my sights.

I didn't check to see if Matt had followed, but I hoped he would be sober enough to move quickly when he needed to.

I approached the guards. I swung my hips from side to side as I shifted my weight, waiting for their attention to naturally turn to me.

When they both looked up from their phones, I slapped the devices out of their hands at the same time. As they scrambled to catch the electronics, I backhanded them both, focusing on their noses.

These guys easily had a few feet on me, but hitting someone in the nose made them become useless pretty quickly.

It was that straight bit of cartilage between the eyes that really did the damage. When whacked hard and with purpose, the resulting pain changes any ability to process for a precious few seconds. I gripped them both by the hair and smacked their heads together like wayward bowling balls.

The noise made even me wince. I stripped them of their weapons quickly and checked the chambers to make sure they were properly loaded. I had two machine guns and two pistols, plus a knife.

I slung a few over my shoulder like deadly purses and the

others I tucked in my various pockets. These uniforms that Max's men wore were fantastic for holding weapons.

I used the zip ties one of my unconscious guards had in his chest pocket to tie them both to each other.

Matt accepted the ties I tossed to him and worked on their legs.

Once I was comfortable they were staying put, I tried to calculate how long I had until they both had reinforcements. I was under no delusions that this whole scene wasn't on camera.

Max wouldn't even have a blind spot in his surveillance. The casino aspect alone was a game changer—add to all his dirty dealings and I might as well have been filming a *Star Wars* mini-series in here with all the footage I was sure he had.

"Um. I didn't catch what you said you did for a living?" Max stepped over the larger guard as I inched forward.

"Probably because I didn't tell you. Unless you're a mind reader, Matt. Are you spiritually gifted, my friend?" I stopped at the large vent instead of walking through the now open door.

I used a knife sitting on the food cart to unscrew the bolts in the wall. Matt picked up another butter knife and added to my efforts.

"I'm not gifted at all. Can't even get out of my own damn way." He dropped the screw he'd loosened on the floor and together we lifted the vent cover and set it aside.

I peeked into the vent. It would fit us if we hunched. I stepped inside and Matt followed. I pictured the layout in my mind. The blueprints to this particular building had been etched in my mind while I'd practiced and reviewed the plans we had for this very shakedown.

"Indy."

I turned left and then right, following my own harshly whispered name.

Aster came around the corner in an outfit very similar to mine.

"Hey."

Leto scrambled from behind Aster and grabbed his brother up in a hug. "Matt! Shit, I was sure I was going to die trying to get you out of here."

Matt slapped his brother on the back. "I knew you'd find me, bro. You never give up."

Zinny flashed a light past me. "We don't have long. They're going to be onto all of us soon."

I knew she was right. "Z, take these fools down to the cars. Get them out of our hair."

I tossed her a knife because she had a few guns already.

Leto looked from Zinny to me and back again.

"Wait, what?" He pointed at me and then back at Aster.

"We have other things to do, baby. Get going. I got you your brother as a present. Go hide for the rest of your lives." I sidestepped and reached a hand out. Sure enough, I was able to grasp the step of a ladder. This was how we would get back to Max.

"You're the Lady Mafia? The like, actual Lady Mafia?" Leto's face seemed strained, like he was trying to do long division while sinking in quicksand.

I rolled my eyes. "No. We're just drunk randos on a plane that you kidnapped. And we happen to know the layout of this building. And the way to bury a ton of mercenaries."

Leto stepped closer to me. "All this time? I had you? I was totally in the right!"

"Or we needed a way to get into the building, and you provided it. Now get lost. I don't have patience for much more of this." I started to climb the ladder and thought better of it. I reached back down and grabbed Leto by the throat. "You sound the alarm, and you'll have me on your case for the rest of your very short, miserable life. I'm ten steps ahead of you and one hundred percent trained to kill your ass."

I waited to make sure Leto's eyes recognized what I was saying. I got that he was still dealing with a bit of shock, but we didn't have time to let him have a revelation.

I released his neck and reached for the next step. I needed to get Max and get the hell out of here with my girls.

Aster came with me as Zinny motioned for the men to follow her. It was a quick transition, but if anyone could whip those men in line, it was Zinny.

A light illuminated the vent and I mumbled thanks to Aster. I knew she would have a way to see in the dark. First, because she hated it, and second, because she was pretty skilled at planning ahead—if you left out the shrimping habit she had.

When we got to the top of the vent, the air ducts were much, much smaller. I hated this part. And hanging out in bad people's ceilings was something I found myself doing way more than I wanted to.

Aster patted my butt. "Hang in there, Indy."

She knew I had a touch of claustrophobia. I pushed myself into the tight space and wiggled forward. Both my shoulders were touching the sides of the air duct. I felt the panic race through me like it was on a track headed for the finish line.

I knew Aster would be fine. She could hide in a hole for days. The tighter, the better. As long as she had a light source, she was like a ground spider.

Speaking of spiders, I was doing my best not to react to the webs I was pushing through. No heebie-jeebies.

"How many?" I paused in my forward motion.

"Two more. We passed three. You've got this." Aster rubbed my ankle.

She was talking about the spot for the air filters. Each room had one we had to crawl over.

I pushed forward a touch more and felt my shoulders inch closer to my neck. It was narrowing. The vent was getting smaller.

Fixating on the distance, I felt my vision tunneling.

In my childhood, there was a bunch of crap I worked hard not to think about. The slow squeezing of my space was one of them. The flashbacks roared through my head like a train. After a steadying breath, I clamped them out. Just zen. Just my girls and me. We were unstoppable.

Aster said nothing as I stayed motionless. That was the thing about knowing each other this long. She knew no amount of encouragement would get me through the flashback any sooner. We both had to wait it out.

I pushed forward again. Locking out my fears—old ones and the ones that hung on like koala bears despite the time I had put in away from them.

Finally, we were at the correct vent. I lifted out the filter silently and pushed it down the vent. Now I could see what I was dealing with. This would be a messy swing in. Max was still in the room and he was watching monitors with a few of his guys.

I watched as his jaw tightened and a vein in his forehead jumped. Other than that, he was cool as a cucumber.

"So we have a few women down in the casino and the cops are on route?" He pointed to one of the screens with his pinkie finger.

"That's right, sir. And it looks like, I mean, right here if we back it up, a car takes off out of the parking lot. We don't know where they are or who they were." I could see the sweat on the bearer of bad news' forehead from here.

"And the woman we had downstairs? Indy?"

"We checked, sir. The guards were knocked out and she was long gone. With Matt." After delivering the bad news, the guy took a big step backward.

Max punched the wall next to him. Once, twice, and then a third time. There was blood after the first punch, so I knew we were dealing with someone that was possibly psychotically enraged. The quiet ones were always sneaky, and Max had a reputation of being very, very deadly.

I held a hand out behind me, and Aster placed a small pair of goggles in it. After sliding them on, I put my hand back and counted down from three to one on my fingers so Aster would be ready. We had to use the element of surprise and we had to move soon. The air vents would be where I'd look if I had an escapee. And I was betting it'd be where these guys would go, once they stopped focusing on the cars that left. We slipped on our masks before we moved in.

I dove through the vent, using my body weight to destroy the clamps that normally held the vent in place. I tumbled into a front flip and landed superhero style on the floor.

Aster had hefted a smoke grenade in just as I fell, so the men inside wouldn't be able to aim at me with their guns. Instead of following me into the room, she would set up in the ceiling with her pistol. She had a suppressor on it, so we could take care of business.

And in the smoke I worked. The goggles I had put on earlier also let me see better.

I went low and took out two of the guys. Aster had hit them with a high-powered dart in their necks and foreheads respectively. We weren't trying for a massacre. There was no need to develop yet another war in the mafia world.

We needed Max. Preferably alive.

When the smoke cleared, Max was standing in the center of the room. I pulled my goggles up and patted him down. I inspected as he took in the attack. It was just Aster and me, and I watched as the realization that we were the actual Lady Mafia dawned on him.

"You were here the whole time." Max put his hands on his head as I directed him to. Aster swung into the room like the gymnast she was in high school.

She zip tied the guys on the ground. They would be out for hours, but we were always better safe than sorry.

"Mercy says hi." I pulled his arms behind his back and secured them with a zip tie as well. Mercy was the alias of the man I was working with. His face had a skull tattoo and his reputation was larger than life.

Max turned his head so he could look at me. "That'll be the last thing he says."

Aster snapped her forefinger on the syringe to make sure there were no bubbles in the sedative.

"Doubt it." Then she inserted the needle into Max's neck.

I helped ease him to the ground. "I thought we were waiting to sedate him until we had him in the cart?"

"Shit. Sorry. The shrimpies you know." Aster moved past me, already onto our next step.

She opened the door to Max's office, and Zinny was waiting there with a laundry cart.

"Did the guys go?" I helped her wheel it in and lay it on its side.

It took all three of us to stuff Max inside and right the cart.

"Yeah. Well, I heard the cars leave, but I wasn't sure how long you would take. Or if you would freeze up in the vent like normal." Zinny pulled the mask up over her face again.

"Are we headed to the roof?" Aster grabbed a few more weapons and we all took a look at the surveillance monitors.

We watched as four of Max's men burst onto the roof, wielding their guns.

"If Mercy had let me kill those guys, rather than playing footsie, we *could* go to the roof. Instead, I think we need to take the service elevator and get a car. We can meet up with the helicopter a few miles away." Zinny kicked the laundry cart.

"Maybe don't complain, Z. We get the job done and then we retire. We can't define the details of the job." I saw a camper in the service garage.

"Is this the bottom floor of that parking garage?" I tapped on the screen as Aster felt Max for a pulse.

Zinny nodded. "Yeah. We could possibly get there, but I'm pretty sure I'm going to have to kill a few people."

Aster threw a couple of pillows from Max's sofa and a plush blanket over his crumpled form.

"Last resort, Z. I mean it."

Zinny had anger problems. And considering that she'd slept

with Aster's fiancé, our retirement was going to start out in a pretty significant fight.

She nodded once. I knew she trusted me. And I trusted Nix/Mercy that we needed to keep people alive.

"Roll out."

Aster pushed the cart, and Z and I made sure the path was clear. Once we got to the elevator, Z pushed the button.

I had a brief moment of panic as I tried to remember what floors this particular elevator stopped at.

Maybe it *was* time for retirement. I should have no trouble pulling up those details.

I had to believe that one of these two girls remembered what I didn't.

The elevator arrived, and no one was in it. This was the part I wasn't thrilled about. We were about to be vulnerable and trapped for at least five floors.

After we were in the elevator with the cart, I pressed the ground level button. We would be in the dark—not literally—thankfully for Aster, but I wouldn't know what we were facing until the doors slid open.

We waited as the floors ticked by. The things that could go wrong roared through my head. Anyone else calling the elevator would stop it on the descent. The fact that the pile of bodies we left in Max's office was bound to be found. The mercenaries on the roof would soon know that we'd made our escape, and I could practically smell their determination to find us again.

We all moved to the side to provide ourselves with a modicum of shelter when the doors opened, yet we would still be easy targets in this elevator. And whoever on the other side could have serious firepower.

When I finally peeked out of the open doors when the elevator stopped, I was surprised to see Leto standing there holding a gun.

I turned to Zinny. "I thought he was gone?"

She shook her head. "He *was* gone. But too stupid to stay away."

We rolled the cart off the elevator and heard clamoring feet above us.

Aster's eyes tracked the noise. "We've been made."

I stepped closer to Leto and his gun aimed at my chest. "Are you coming with us, or are you dying?"

Zinny rolled her eyes. For her, there was one choice, and it wasn't his to make.

With Leto's attention on me, he didn't notice as Aster slipped behind him and jammed a needle in his neck. Zinny slapped the gun out of his hand at the exact moment. I pushed the cart as Leto fell and the girls hefted his feet into the cart on top of Max's unconscious, lumped up form. And we were off, running.

I prayed as we reached the truck. Now that we were next to it, I was guessing the casino sent its linens out to be cleaned, because this was a big laundry truck. The back door swung open and Aster hollered in delight.

"Keys are in it!"

Zinny hopped into the truck and pushed out the ramp. These very carts and this truck were meant to work together. Once I had the cart lined up, Aster had to jump out of the truck and help us push the cart into the back. I noticed she had taken the time to sling a weapon on her back—they were getting closer, for sure.

Zinny crawled in the back and slammed the doors shut, closing herself in with our prisoners.

Knowing each other for as long as we did, the beauty was that we didn't have to speak in times like this. Aster would drive—as long as she wasn't high on shrimp, she was the best at it.

I would be our eyes and navigator. We were headed out of the parking garage when the gunshots began pinging around us.

Our tiny flip phone was already on the console. Aster had the thing hidden in her body, but the condom she used to smuggle it was removed.

I tried not to think about how many other things she had in her special "dick wallet" as she called it.

She claimed her Kegels were so on point she could smuggle a bowling ball. I never wanted to know the specifics.

I kept my eyes on the side view mirror as Aster crashed the garage arm that monitored exits effectively.

"We've got vehicles."

I worried about Zinny in the back with just thin metal to protect her from possible bullets.

Aster spun the wheel and slammed the gas pedal so we were headed west.

"Last job. We lose no one." I wasn't sure if I was notifying Aster or the universe.

"You got it." Aster was pressing the truck to go as fast as it could.

I hit the programmed number in the cell phone as I lowered the passenger side window.

"Extraction requested. Coming in hot."

Another female assassin responded coolly, like I had placed a lunch order. "How hot?"

"Super spicy." I ended the call and made sure the phone was broadcasting our signal. We had to survive long enough to get to a place where the helicopter could land.

"I got a place." Aster careened hard to the right and I aimed out of the window while our broadside was exposed. We had four SUVs and two motorcycles bearing down on us.

"Shit." The SUVs weren't the problem. I mean, they were hard to deal with, but the crotch rockets were fast and nimble. The drivers knew what they were doing. As I aimed, one of the motorcycles damn near laid flat as they leaned into the hard turn.

I was able to hit the tire of the first SUV and he spun out, clipping the second SUV. The other motorcycle maneuvered around the crash like he did it all day. These guys were really, really good.

Aster turned again, getting our enemies behind us.

"The way they are shooting at us makes me think..." Aster started.

"...that they don't know we have Max," I finished for her.

They would never be this reckless.

"Or they do and they want him dead." Aster was driving like this was her hometown. I loved her photographic memory when it came to maps.

"There's always a chance of that with these kinds of men." I was able to get off two more shots, but neither hit.

I heard the drumbeat of helicopter blades in the distance.

Our ride was coming. Aster merged onto a long, straight road. There were just a few cars, but they made us concerned. We had a one hundred percent accuracy with our hits. We'd never taken out an innocent bystander in the past, and we didn't want to start now.

"I'm going to line them up pretty for T." I used my gunfire to herd the SUVs and the motorcycles into a fairly straight line behind us.

The good news about a long, straight road was a helicopter could land on it. The bad news was it gave the motorcycles plenty of room to gobble pavement.

The helicopter's blades were getting so loud, I felt like it was driving a rhythm into my bloodstream.

One after another, the SUVs peeled away with various, dramatic problems. We had cover from the sky. I slipped back into the vehicle.

"T's lighting it up out there." I checked the side mirror and it was blasted off the truck.

"Somebody back there is still holding up." I watched as Aster clenched the steering wheel harder, preparing for anything she could dream of. Exploded tires, wild shots—it could be anything.

I looked to the side mirror, even though it was no longer there. I was shocked by the appearance of the motorcycle driver looking back at me.

"Duck!" I leaned back as he took aim with his gun.

Aster lurched to the left and swerved at the same time. The motorcycle was clipped and went out of control.

"You okay?" I put my hand on Aster's shoulder.

She sat up and checked her mirror. "Yeah. That was close."

"How's it looking now?" I didn't want to stick my head out of the window to look.

"Clear for the moment. I bet they have reinforcements coming, though."

A text pinged on my phone.

Landing.

"Pull to a stop. Let's see if we still have Z back there." I pointed to the stretch of pavement in front of us.

Aster did as I asked, and I was out of the truck before the wheels came to a full stop.

The rear truck door was pulled open and I was relieved to see Zinny crouched next to the two men.

"You okay?" I hopped into the back. The men were tied up and had duct tape over their mouths. Both had their eyes closed.

"Yeah. We'll talk about who rides in the back next time, because I think I just earned myself out of ever having to do it again."

The helicopter landing behind us cut out any more conversation.

I was wondering if we should put the guys back in the laundry cart, but two burly guys sprang off of the helicopter as T stood watch on the road behind us all.

Aster came around the truck and gave a relieved huff as she saw Zinny.

Both Max and Leto were put into fireman carries and we hustled behind them. T started shooting, so we knew that it was a tight time frame.

Aster and Zinny scrambled into the cabin of the helicopter.

66

They turned as the copter started to lift off. My girls each extended an arm and I grabbed hold.

They yanked me in as the road disappeared below us. Zinny slammed the helicopter door shut.

This helicopter was designed to carry cargo and just two people, so we were all sitting on the floor, save for T, who was still aiming at the cars pursuing us, and the pilot and the co-pilot.

In just a few minutes, T slammed her door shut. "They can't get to us now."

She set her gun down after pulling on the safety.

"We're over woods for a while now, right?" She hollered to the pilot.

He nodded in response.

The helicopter was a loud ride. T slumped down next to me. I greeted her with a nod while I evaluated her. She wasn't injured in any way I could see by the firefight.

She had more in common with Aster, Zinny, and me than most other people in this world. Female assassins, raised in foster care that had grown into wildly deadly adult women were a small subset of the population.

Her involvement with the second in command in her organization was a blurred line. They were really both equally in charge. The head of the joint was a guy who went by the name of Mercy, but we knew him by his real name, Nix.

Even though he was completely covered in a detailed skeleton tattoo, he was now a family man. What can I say? The ladies and I had interesting friends.

Max had been placed facedown on the floor, so I could look at his spider tattoo.

I pulled out my phone and scrolled through the few pictures on it until I had the image I was looking for. The spider tattoo and placement were identical to the one Nix had sent me.

This one sells girls. I need him.

Nix had handpicked the Lady Mafia for this job. Not because he and his team couldn't do it, but he understood the lovely sense of irony that an all lady team would take this fucker in.

I was blaming him having a six-month-old daughter for his understanding on where Aster, Zinny, and I stood on that particular crime.

A smile tugged at the corners of my mouth as I imagined Max regaining consciousness. We'd been baiting him for over a year. Planting things, making sure that he had a real ax to grind against the Lady Mafia.

As the helicopter descended toward the airport, I felt the vibrations of the engine rumbling. I expected that the next leg of our journey was within sight when I stood to see. A rustic coffin was set up. I looked at T.

She shrugged. It was the easiest way to travel with an unconscious person.

I watched as her gaze flitted between Max and Leto and back again.

I didn't have a good reason for keeping Leto. In my heart, I knew it was because I figured Max's guys would kill him and I wanted him to have a proper reunion with his brother. I was a sucker for sibling reunions.

I shrugged back at T. I couldn't explain all that over the racket of blades as they slowed down. She gave me the hand signal, holding up two fingers.

I knew what she wanted to know. Were we taking both on the next leg? I gave her one nod in the affirmative.

I met Zinny's raised eyebrow and Aster's smirk by rolling my eyes. They would be on my case for stealing the hot suit guy.

But I really wanted the kidnapper to have to become the kidnapped for a few hours. At least that was what I was telling myself.

The burly men helped load the coffin with both Max and Leto. It was a tight fit, but laying them on their sides, spoon style, was the key.

I noticed that the coffin was equipped with some air holes, so chances were they would be fine on the plane.

T came with us after briefly talking to the helicopter pilots. We now had three big guys, my girls, T, and the coffin loaded onto the private plane.

The big guys acted like pallbearers, bridging the coffin up the plane stairs.

The inside was set up like a plush living room and we each chose a place to collapse. We were rolling down the runway almost right away. They'd been waiting for us.

T took out her phone and tapped out a text message. Then she focused her brown eyes on me. "How'd that go?"

"Well enough." It had been our most public assignment yet. And hopefully our last.

Zinny stretched her hands above her head. "You guys have a shower when we land?"

Aster redid her ponytail, smoothing the hair around her face back into the hair tie.

"Yeah. You can clean up there." T picked up the phone and spoke into it. "Yeah, did some damage. Can you monitor for any police activity, though I bet he has paid off more than a few. We may not have to worry about official blowback. Can you tell Bossman that we have one extra?"

She listened for a bit, and a deep voice was buzzing for a bit in her ear. I couldn't make out what was being said, but the unflappable T had a slight blush and then she ended the call.

There was a reason we liked working with Mercy's crew. They were professional and not assholes. But either way, this was it. We were out. Last score to pad the retirement funds, then the girls and I were going our separate ways—well, first we were going to get Aster married, or we had been going to.

I hadn't gotten to ask Zinny if claiming that sleeping with Aster's fiancé was part of the act. I had a hunch that it wasn't.

Zinny hated how much Aster relied on her shrimp hack to

keep the man happy. And if he loved her—as far as Zinny was concerned—it shouldn't matter what size her boobs were.

Zinny was right, but I also knew Aster was hard-headed. And sometimes she would sink in if someone told her not to do something.

I watched both of them for a minute and then swallowed. Splitting up—it's what made the most sense. We'd done a lot of damage; we'd completed a ton of jobs. Splitting up after this job was the most sensible thing. This type of job had a shelf life, and most people didn't live past the expiration date.

We lied on a regular basis, but our love for each other was as real as anything. We'd met in foster care—all the same age, but from different backgrounds. We were enrolled in the small school —all in the same class. Our reputation was soon firmed up. We protected the girls. It's what we did. If a boy was harassing someone, they faced us. On the playground, one would distract the teacher and the other two would dole out the punishments.

The good news was the boys learned. Soon, all a girl had to do was invoke our name and the boys would mind their business.

And then as we aged, we kept it up. Hell, we got a taste for it. As we aged out of placement, we stuck together. Teen girls with no home to call their own were vulnerable. In a group we were safer. We were also angry. Angry at things that we separately faced before we were a group.

The fights had been had. Aster was getting married. Zinny wanted to branch out. If I was being honest, I knew she had a taste for killing that wasn't healthy. Okay, fine. Having any kind of taste was not great, but I always had revenge or retribution to comfort me.

Aster was ready for driving a minivan and dancing to TikToks with her kids someday. She was willing to kill herself to make it happen. I ran my hands over my head, trying to keep the headache from forming there.

I was feeling like I was losing control. I didn't want to do this anymore, but I didn't want to lose my girls either. They were the only family I claimed.

We locked eyes, our gaze lingering for a moment. I didn't say anything, but she was the kind of person that read energy and body language really easily. I might ask her opinion on the whole thing if I got a chance. It was a weird position to be in, and she might be able to understand better than anyone else.

I tipped the chair back and hit the button to raise my feet. This was a safe place to turn off my defenses. It happened fairly rarely, so I pushed my concerns away and let sleep take me.

CHAPTER
FOURTEEN

Being spooned was so comforting. It was a great way to slowly wake up. The dark was great, too. Hotel rooms were amazing with their blackout curtains. And I must have had a hell of a night because my head was pounding. I gradually became more aware. The noise was comforting at first—a loud, white static. Almost like a jet plane.

And then I felt the gentle bouncy bump like a plane. I slowly opened my eyes, letting them adjust. This was a small space. A really small space. A too small space. My adrenaline and heart rate spiked immediately. I was being spooned. Spooned by—I lay still —a man, guessing from the stick I had lodged in my ass crack.

I tried to open my mouth to holler, but it was taped shut. Shit. Shit.

It came back, first out of focus, and then so sharply the memories felt like they scarred the inside of my head. Indy, Aster, and Zinny. They were the real Lady Mafia! I felt my eyes go wide. A small fire of pride stupidly flared. I found them! And then it was extinguished. Because really, they had found me. I was just a pawn. The elevator flashed back to me. Seeing the ladies. I was there to help them. I wanted to make sure they got out alive. And what did I get for having chivalry? Well, I was in a tight box with a groaning man. Judging from how much he was muted, I was guessing he had tape on his mouth as well.

There was a little bit of light near the top of my head. I tilted up and saw that there were tiny holes. That gave me some peace of mind because that meant I'd at least have air. I tried not to let panic overtake me as I realized how vulnerable I was in this little box.

Shit. Someone was messing with the box, sliding it and shifting it. The man behind me started trying to shout and move, smashing my knees into the walls.

I tried shouting back, but all I was able to convey was, "Moopp!"

I made my body as rigid as possible and used my feet to help me push him against the wall a little. I wasn't trying to get in a fist-fight with my hands tied behind my back in a box, but I was also not interested in having this guy panic the fuck out and hurt us both.

The lid to the box opened, and as it did, my pupils were flooded with light. My head was pounding even more. I blinked to try to focus.

Meatheads. Three giant meatheads were standing over the box, which I now realized was a coffin, looking at us.

Honestly, the fact that I was in a coffin was tripping me out. It was off-putting and panic inducing. And I wasn't even alone in my coffin.

Next, I saw Indy's beautiful face. She looked over my situation and wrinkled her nose. "Sorry, they were only expecting one. Can you get him out of there, please?"

The meatheads shrugged and nodded. Two of them lifted me out like I was a trash bag and deposited me onto the floor. Indy knelt down next to me and ripped off my mouth tape.

While holding out her hand, she asked, "Anybody got a pocket knife?"

Meathead Number Two opened his up and passed it to her handle side in.

She used her fingers to create a bit of slack and began hacking through the zip tie. When I was finally free, I realized how tight they had been. The blood rushed into my fingers as I rubbed my hands.

"You alright? " She stood and held out her hand.

I took it and she helped me stand up. I turned to see Max getting closed back in the coffin, his eyes closing. Meathead Number Three had a spent syringe in his hand. Max was sedated again, I assumed.

At least I was out. "Are these your guys?"

I still felt the sting of betrayal even though it had no place in my head. Hell, I'd kidnapped these ladies, I couldn't pretend that I was angry that they were actually who everyone was looking for.

She shook her head. "Nope. They work for someone else. The same person I'm working for. Do you want to come sit up here? I've got a water."

She waved her hand in the direction of the seating area. Zinny, Aster, and another woman were all looking me over.

Zinny smiled and gave me the middle finger. "If it was up to me, you'd be dead a few times already."

"Thanks. Thanks for that." I took the fancy bottle of water Indy passed to me. I opened it and rehydration instantly consumed me. I was done in a sloppy hurry. Indy passed me a second bottle.

"Maybe take a breath," she offered as advice.

I ignored her and chugged down the next bottle—this time it was carbonated water. As soon as I set down the empty bottle, I felt the hard burp rising in my chest. I had swallowed too much water and bubbles.

I covered my mouth and tried to let the burp out as quietly as possible.

"Told ya." Indy shifted in her seat on the couch next to me.

I wiped my mouth and leaned back. My brain was still fuzzy from the drugs. I could tell that now that my adrenaline had subsided.

"Bringing a pet with you is not encouraged." Zinny gave Indy a hard glare.

Indy sucked in her cheeks in annoyance. "Mind your business, Z."

So I was a sore spot already. Great. "Where are we headed?"

My voice was scratchy and I leaned back against the couch.

All the women were silent.

"Okay. Good info. Nice talk." I crunched the water bottle in my hands.

"We've got another hour." The woman I didn't know directed the information at Indy, but I was happy to know we were close to done with whatever this was.

Aster started sobbing.

"Shit." Indy got up and knelt by Aster's chair. "What's going on?"

Aster took the tissue the other woman offered. "Nothing. It's nothing. Just having the pre-wedding hormones."

"I don't think that's a thing," Zinny observed dryly.

"Why don't you just hump them then? See if the hormones like you better than me?" Aster bit her lips together.

"I thought we had this fight and were done with it already?" Zinny looked at her nails. "And hormones are not humpable."

Indy clenched her jaw while her foot tapped. "We're still not in a great place to discuss a personal matter. Can we wait until we're done with Mercy?"

I was really hoping no one was done with having mercy when it came to me. Being kidnapped instead of being the kidnapper certainly changed my perspective in a hurry.

Aster blew her nose. "Sure, baby. I'll keep it together for you."

Indy stood and patted Aster's shoulder. Then she walked over to Zinny, leaned over, and harshly whispered in her ear. Zinny grimaced at Indy but stopped asking questions.

The rest of the plane ride I felt like I had cotton in my mouth. Eventually, one of the Meatheads showed me the bathroom and I peed forever.

I wasn't sure what was going on here. I was glad that I wasn't in the coffin anymore with Max, but it wasn't like I was a free man. When I was done in the bathroom, we began our descent. We all buckled our seatbelts that were hidden in the plush chairs.

The pilot was very skilled and the landing was as smooth as glass.

When we stopped, the Lady Mafia strapped themselves back up with guns. When they all turned to look at me, I was concerned.

Zinny pointed at me with her pinkie. "Shouldn't your new toy be in the coffin with Max?"

My eyes darted to the quiet box near the door.

Indy clicked her tongue. "I've got him, Z. If he does anything wrong, I'll shoot him."

With that, the door was opened and the stairs were deployed. Indy walked next to me.

I leaned my head toward her. "You're going to shoot me?"

"Not in the head or anything." Indy slipped her arm in mine.

"Is this considered a date then?" I lifted my eyebrows.

I was rewarded with a half-smile, but otherwise she didn't respond.

We were loaded into the SUVs and Max and his coffin were slid into their own SUV. Aster joined the driver of the hearse. Indy seemed to finally relax.

"Why is this better?" I made a circle with my index finger.

"What?" She gave me a side-eye.

"You were more stressed on the plane, and now that we're in the back of this SUV, your whole demeanor is more chill." Indy's jaw wasn't tense anymore and her foot had stopped tapping.

"Because we unleashed all of Max's men on ourselves. And they know what you look like, too. So I wanted to make sure we got to Mercy's compound without any more drama. These SUVs are equipped like they are for the President, so I know we're fairly safe. And I'm close to mission accomplished." She crossed her legs. Why did she look so good in a simple grunt uniform?

"So the mission was to bring Max to this place?" I was asking leading questions, but maybe it was because I was confused how the three women that were complete debacles wound up playing both Max and me so thoroughly.

"Don't pry. It's not polite." She rested her head back on the seat.

"Of course. Pardon me. You threatening to shoot me is a show of perfect manners, though?" I turned to look at her and her eyes were closed. She was actually catching a nap.

I should be trying to figure out a way out of this place. Contact my guys, check on my brother, but dammit if I didn't follow her lead and try to sleep off some more of this drug hangover.

CHAPTER
FIFTEEN

When the SUV stopped, I was curled up against Leto's chest like a cat. I had my hand threaded under his shirt, resting on his abs. I was fully snuggled in. His arm was draped around my shoulders and his hand was holding my left boob.

When I pushed away, he came to as well. He released my breast and his eyes went wide. "Whoa. Sorry. Damn. Sorry."

I slid back over to my side of the back seat and caught Lock's amused gaze in the rearview mirror.

Lock was married to Mercy's sister and he was a giant wiseass. I knew he would give me crap about Leto when he got a chance.

The compound that Mercy worked from was close to his real residence. He liked to be able to get home and play with his kid. But this part was all business. There were fences and cameras everywhere. He was known for surveillance and took it seriously.

I opened the door and motioned for Leto to follow me out. Aster was joking with her driver and Zinny was talking to T when we finally assembled on the stairs.

T's husband, Animal, came to the door and opened it. She stepped up to him and he leaned down to give her a deep kiss. She eventually pushed away, laughing. Seeing her with him was always cute. She went from stone-cold killer to soft and shy.

As some of the guys played pallbearers again, we stepped to the side so Max would be encased in the security of the house.

After we were all in the living room, Max's coffin was opened again. Zinny checked his pulse and nodded to me. Max was alive, and as his eyes popped open, I mentally added the adjective 'kicking' to his description.

Indy took a step back and two of Mercy's larger guys moved forward. Max stopped kicking.

He had been the head of the dirty Casino for so long, he had to have some good instincts. And going quiet was his best one yet today.

Mercy entered the room with his hood pulled up over his head. I walked over to Max at the same time he did.

"Nice work." His voice was low, but he was pleased. I could tell from the way he rubbed his fingers together that he was hoping I'd be successful. "Max, welcome to my place. We have a bunch to talk about." Mercy lifted his hood away from his face. I'd seen his face tattoos quite a few times, but it was still a slight surprise to the system every time. His face, having the dark marks of a skull, was very disquieting.

Animal came up behind us. "The tattoo?"

Mercy nodded at the men next to us. They stepped forward and rolled Max like a rotisserie chicken so they could see his hand.

"That's the tattoo." Mercy tilted his head one way and then the other.

Animal smiled. "We got him. We can juice him like a lemon for all the info we need downstairs. Guys, bag him up."

Max's eyes were frantic. He looked from me to Mercy to Animal and back. He wanted to have some say in what was happening.

I was betting he was getting a small taste of what the girls he trafficked felt when they were in his organization, and that was what I liked to call karma.

When the coffin was removed, Mercy motioned for me to come with him into his office. Zinny came closer.

She may be angry with me, but she'd never abandon me.

Animal held up a hand. "Baby doll, it's okay. She's safe, I promise."

He had a way about him that just diffused a situation and instilled confidence in those around him. It worked on Zinny.

Aster was still busy talking to the tall brown-haired guard that had been driving her SUV. He was handsome, and I was hoping she was practicing flirting on someone else besides Spenser.

I followed Mercy as he held the door for me. I walked in and he closed the door behind me. He had a wall of surveillance monitors that held a steady eye on every room in the place. I naturally found the screen with the most motion, and it included the coffin and the men I had just witnessed.

Mercy motioned for me to sit, and I took a seat.

"How'd it go?" He steepled his hands, also marked with bones in ink.

"Well, he's here." The rundown would take a while.

"And we have an extra guy here? Care to tell me what that was all about?" He leveled me with his hard gaze.

"He's my responsibility. None of it will kick back on you." I shifted in my chair.

"Hey, I trust you, Indy, but I'm going to need to know where we're going with this. How did he wind up in my living room?" Mercy leaned forward a bit.

"I'm not sure. It's a gut impulse. If we left him, he would have been killed. He was really worried about his brother, Matt. Max had him captive, and we managed to free Matt because he was literally in the same place as I was. So I wanted them to have that reunion. And then he came back to the casino, so we drugged him and brought him." It was sounding weak, and I was really having a time trying to sound reasonable.

"Let's talk to him for a minute." Mercy stood and opened the door. In no time, Leto was coming in, standing in a spot near me on the couch.

"Sir. Great to meet you. I'm Leto, and I've heard good things." Leto stuck out his hand for a shake.

Mercy rolled his eyes. "I bet it wasn't good things, my dude." He reluctantly shook Leto's hand.

"Well, good has a sliding scale. I just know that your reputation is solid." He sat down on the couch next to me.

"How's your headache?" I squinted at him. He looked like he was recovering nicely. Aster was a master of dosing, so I was confident he'd be fine.

"Fading. Thanks for asking." Leto looked at me from my eyes to my lips and back.

"So, Leto, tell me how you and your brother came to be involved in the casino business today." Mercy flashed his attention to the monitors on the walls as if seeing everything and watching all things was second nature.

Leto thought for a few moments. I was pretty good at spotting liars, and I would have bet money that Leto was telling the truth as he shared his story.

"My brother is shit at making bets. He takes chances when he shouldn't. He believes he's a winner no matter what. This time around, he got involved with Max, and that loan had a very high interest rate, if you know what I mean." Leto plucked at his pants.

"That explains him. How about you?" Mercy focused back on Leto.

"My uncle. I got in the business from my uncle. When my dad passed, my uncle offered Matt and me jobs to help support my mom and our sisters. So we became bag men for my uncle's contingent. Teens could do the job, and we did. We had a broken down taxi that was shit but ran. And we would take money from one place to another. We'd sit there, listen for a code word, and pass the money through the window. It paid good. And Ma and our sisters could have the stuff they needed." Leto shook his head. "But need and want are the same damn thing for my brother. And he wanted more. He wanted our sisters in college. He wanted Mom in a new car. So he started interacting more with the clients that we were meeting. I would've been fine—staying just bag men. You can get out of being bag men. Once you start doing real jobs? There's no getting out. I mean, I'm sure you know that."

Leto bit his bottom lip, and I could almost see him weighing his words. As he told his story, he was filtering on the fly as he informed the boss of a mafia.

He didn't know what I did about Mercy. He was actually a good guy. A fucked-up good guy, but he had a heart.

"I couldn't let my brother get into that life without having backup, so I was backup. I took the harder jobs and he got addicted to gambling. I had to keep my sisters in school, Mom in her house, and my brother clear of debts." Leto looked at his feet.

"That's a hell of a place to be in." Mercy observed calmly.

"It sure felt like one. And then he started doing jobs for Max and immediately turning his money into the casino. While I was away in the Army, things escalated. And then he'd take the long way to drop off a bag and stop to gamble it. Sometimes he killed at it. Doubling what was in the bag, and no one was wiser. But then he started losing. And losing. So his debt was huge. Then Max took him, and that's pretty much where we are now. I hired some guys to help me get the Lady Mafia. I wanted to swap the real crew for my brother. You know, to pay his debt with finding them. But then, I just wanted to be in the building with him. Get a chance to bust him out. And that's when I met the ladies. Indy here got him out as a side quest, and then she kidnapped Max. The biggest boss in town." He turned his attention to me, and I saw the respect there.

I knew I was good at what I did, but it made me happy that Leto had noticed it. This was why it was good not to catch feelings. I was getting older. When I was younger, I would have never had mushy thoughts about a guy.

"That's what they do. The impossible. That's why they got the job." Mercy looked past Leto to me. "Do you believe him?"

"Yes, I do. I think he can lie, but he's not lying about this. What do you think?" I wanted to see if I was being blinded by his gorgeous freaking eyes.

Mercy nodded. "Agreed. I think he's a liar and will lie but is truthful right now."

"This doesn't feel like a ringing endorsement, but I'm grateful either way." Leto lifted his shoulders and rubbed his fingertips together.

"I need to speak to Indy and the other ladies alone now." Mercy pointed at the door.

Leto hesitated for a brief moment, then went to the door. In the next minute, Aster and Zinny came into the office. Zinny shut the door behind her.

Mercy finally let himself smile. "Well done, ladies."

Zinny and Aster settled on the couch next to me. Aster reached out her hand and held mine.

"You're welcome. What's next?" Zinny got straight to the point.

"That's why you're here. I know you said that you were all done and this was the last job. I wanted to know if that was still the case? I can offer you a few more jobs." He held his hands out, palms up.

I knew we had a fracture at the moment. And it had happened before. If we didn't settle back into our default of being a united front, I was concerned any job would be dangerous.

I looked over to Zinny and saw that same answer in her eyes. We had decided it was done. We had to stand on that decision. "We're out, Nix. So sorry."

"Maybe rest, give it some time. You know you can hang here and have a nice time." He rested his hands on his lap.

I tried to read why he would press this.

Aster spoke up, "Let's give it three days. I think that we're entitled to a few days off."

When Aster made a declaration like that, we listened. She was leaning into her intuition.

"Great. I have an empty guest house down by the residence. You're more than welcome to stay there for as long as you'd like." Mercy stood and we did, too. "You have anything with you?"

He motioned to our deadly accessories.

Zinny snorted. "Just guns."

"Animal will order you guys a wardrobe. He's like weirdly good at it." Again, the smile. It was crazy how the skull tattoo melted away after spending some time with Nix.

He went to the door and opened it for us.

On the coffee table I laid out all my weapons, keeping only a knife. I glanced at the monitor. Max was lying on what looked like an operating table. He was unconscious again. More was going on here, and I was actually interested to see why.

When I got to the door, Nix nodded. "You want to keep the guy with you, huh?"

I locked eyes with Leto. "Yeah, I have to figure a few things out."

"Your call." Nix stepped to the side as I entered the living room. "You guys want to have dinner with us tonight?"

It might be nice to have a moment of relaxation with friends. "Sounds good. Just let us know what time."

Animal escorted us all to an SUV and drove us out.

CHAPTER
SIXTEEN

The new part of the Mercy compound was gorgeous. It was like going from a bare bones new construction house to a full-on Disney World. There were rolling hills and topiaries. Statues and ponds—flowers everywhere.

There were houses dotting the whole area, dominated by a mansion in the center.

Animal swerved us into a gorgeous two-story with a circular driveway. After the ladies and I got out, he offered, "I'll have the guys drop off all the necessary items for you. There should be food in the house and stuff to take showers if you want."

Indy grabbed my arm, as Aster shouted, "Biggest!"

Zinny yelled second, "Next!"

"Jerks." Indy moved her mouth to the side.

"Uh, what's going on here?" I leaned down to hear what Indy was going to say.

"When we were all kids, if there was ever a choice of rooms, this is how we settled it." Indy and I followed the other ladies up the stairs.

Zinny held her hand up to the security pad before the door audibly unlocked. After stepping inside, Zinny and Aster took off up the stairs.

"We're not in a rush, because we'll get the worst." Indy and I explored the first floor. There were vaulted ceilings and high windows. Everything was decorated in warm neutrals with pops of orange and red throughout.

"I feel like I stepped into someone's Pinterest dream board." Indy ducked into the kitchen.

The all white number with gold accents was really nice. I opened the fridge and found a cold beer. I grabbed one for Indy and popped the top. I passed it to her and she waited while I opened mine.

"Not sure what the instructions are on recovering from whatever drug Zinny gave you. Like, if it should be completely out of your system before drinking."

I ignored her warning and held up my bottle for a toast. She gave me a look like she wasn't so sure this was the best idea but wasn't about to stop me. We touched the tops of our bottles and both took a swallow.

Then she shouldered past me to see what the huge fridge held. A nice platter of cheese, veggies, and meats was wrapped up on the top shelf. It even had shrimp.

Over my left shoulder, Aster exclaimed, "Yum! A shark coochie board! I need to get a lot of that in my face."

Indy looked over her shoulder to Aster. "No goddamn shrimp."

Zinny arrived in the kitchen. She was still salty and offered, "You know what? Let her blow up like a parade float. Why do we care so much?"

Aster frowned in her direction. "You know what? Screw you, Z. How are you going to give me grief when you slept with my man?"

Indy pulled out the board and set it on the large marble kitchen island. She grabbed the handful of shrimp and walked over to the half bath near the kitchen. We heard a flush and then water running.

Zinny looked under the kitchen sink and found some antibacterial wipes. She plucked out a towel and wiped down the portion of the board the shrimp had been touching. For a lady that said she didn't care what happened to Aster, she was definitely still trying to keep the kitchen contaminate-free.

When Indy returned, she grabbed some plates from inside the cabinet. She set them down next to the board. I got two more beers from the fridge and opened them.

We all started eating like it was our job. I was so hungry that I had to force myself to slow down. It made sense; the last forty-eight hours had been high stress and huge activity. When we were all holding our stomachs, groaning, we seemed to come back to ourselves.

"There are robes and slippers in my bathroom upstairs, so we could all clean up while we wait for clothes?" Aster pointed her finger upstairs.

Zinny put the plates in the sink and left without a word.

Indy and Aster stepped close together.

Aster spoke in a low voice, "Um, she's got a stick up her ass. Do we know why she's clamping onto it so hard?"

Indy looked at the ceiling as we all heard water rushing through the pipes in the house. "I think she's got some hesitancy about retirement. And she's taking it out on you."

Aster tapped her fingers on the countertop. "Wasn't retirement her idea to begin with? I mean, pick a problem and stay in a lane."

Indy nodded. "We'll have to get to the bottom of it with her. For now, I want to see if the shower robe deal holds up for Leto and me."

"We're showering together?" I felt my body perk up.

"No. Not even a little. I just want to see if we have robes and a bathroom or what." Indy headed to the staircase near the half bath.

Aster waited for me to go down behind Indy, and I realized

that they took their positions on purpose. They were still monitoring me. If I made any quick moves, I was pretty sure I would end up facedown with a knife at my neck. It was both hot and scary.

At the bottom of the stairs, the layout of the house had an office and two bedrooms. The Jack and Jill shower was roomy and luxurious. And sure enough, there were slippers and robes folded and set out on the shelves carved into the walkthrough shower.

There was a cabinet that had an array of products to enhance a nice thorough shower.

"Ladies first." I was actually dying to get under a hot stream and work out all these kinks. Lying unconscious snuggled next to Max in a coffin really had me jonesing for a hit of cleanliness.

Indy turned and walked both Aster and me out of the bathroom. When the door was locked, Aster and I looked around the bottom floor. There was a game room, a living room, and a theater. A garage door led us to an empty four-car garage.

"This is a hell of a guest house." I shook my head, thinking about how much money had to be flowing through Mercy's organization.

"Yeah. I can't wait to see the main house. I bet it slaps." Aster sat in one of the theater chairs and I did the same.

"What do you think they're doing to Max?" I was making conversation, but I also wanted to test how deep the ladies were involved with Mercy.

"Nothing good. I'm sure of that. How'd your brother get involved with him, anyway?" She kicked the foot rest out on her chair.

"Matt makes rash choices. Sometimes they work out. But when they don't, he doubles down. It's a cycle I haven't figured out how to put a stop to yet." I pull my feet up as well.

"That's a pretty common personality trait with risk takers." She started pressing buttons on the armrest and the screen in front of us flickered to life. "Oh, I love this show." Aster ignored me and hung on every word as the reality show host asked the woman to decide which of the many men in front of her should receive a rose.

Indy came into the room wrapped in a white robe and her hair in a towel twist. "It's all yours, Hot Suit."

CHAPTER
SEVENTEEN

"We trusting him in there?" Aster pointed after Leto.

"No one gets out of here without Nix knowing, so I think we're good. You want to catch your shower now? I'll babysit the man." I collapsed in a theater seat.

"I do. He told me a bit about his life. FYI: brother is a risk taker and doubles down on bad choices." She pushed up out of her chair.

"Reminds me of someone I know." I lifted an eyebrow at her.

She tried to hide her smile. "Risk takers get shit done. I'll shower, then maybe I'll call Spenser."

Aster headed out and I shouted after her, "Don't call him!"

Aster was stubborn when it came to dating. She was such a catch, but she seemed really set on keeping her relationship with lousy Spenser together.

Zinny walked into the theater room with the same outfit on as me. She took Aster's recently vacated spot.

"She's going to call him." Zinny turned the screen off with her armrest button.

"Yeah. She has to find a phone first. I have the only one." I realized that I didn't have it on me at the moment. And the table where I had left it for my shower was empty.

Zinny shot out of her chair when she put it all together. "You check him, I'll stop her."

I moved as fast as I could in floppy slippers and flung open the bathroom door. I took two huge steps and gathered my now opening robe in my arms.

Leto swung around at my movement. He didn't have the phone.

"She's got it!" I heard Zinny holler from upstairs. And then from the sounds of things, a light wrestling match was getting started.

Leto didn't move to cover up. Once he realized it was me, he went back to soaping up his chest.

"Take a nice long look, honey." He shot a wink at me.

I did my best to avert my eyes, but some things were pretty obvious even in my peripheral vision. He was packing.

"Sorry. False alarm. Continue." I rushed out.

His body was ripped and embedded in my mind. The hairy chest, the trail down to his business parts. A slight smattering of tattoos. The suit wasn't the only thing hot on him.

I stood there looking at a rumpled Zinny holding out my phone. "What'd you find in there?"

She lifted her chin toward the ajar bathroom door.

"A lot. A freaking lot." I slowly shook my head.

"Nice." Both Zinny and I retied our robes.

"Was she on the phone with him?" I was glad that the fight for the phone wasn't still going on.

"No, he sent her to voicemail. The douchebag."

We both kicked our feet out again.

Zinny cleared her throat.

I added, "Before we were so rudely interrupted, I was going to say that I think Aster is trying to force a recreation of a family— once we all retire. She really depends on this."

Zinny sniffled. "Yeah. She's not the only one. Are you thinking of working for Nix some more?"

"I'm not sure about that. I feel like we delivered Max. I wanted to end on a high. We're still young. Plenty of time to..."

"Do what?" Zinny asked like she was actually pointing out something.

"Live a little? We have enough money for a few lifetimes. We're set." I turned in my chair to face her.

"What does set mean, though? Really. We have a job to do. We have a skillset that will go to waste." Zinny had a stranglehold on the armrests, with her knuckles white.

"What we do is illegal, and what we're good at is killing people. That can't be our whole life. Can it? I mean, at some point we have to face that we have a... how did Leto put it? Shelf life. We have a shelf life. Unless you were planning on going and going until we made a mistake that got us killed?" I pulled the towel wrap off my hair and let the wet locks rest on my shoulder.

"You've got it all figured out, right? So decision made. Lady Mafia is dead." Zinny dragged her finger across her throat.

"You've changed your tune. I remember a very different conversation going into this job." She was acting like I had made this decision alone, which I rarely do.

"Yeah, well, after getting done, I see how it will be. How it will become. Aster will get treated like crap from Spenser, and you'll let the next guy in the lineup bone you with his giant schlong. And where does that leave me?" Zinny stood up and pulled her towel hair wrap off as well.

A soft knock came from the doorway into the theater room. Animal had a megawatt smile and armfuls of bags. "Is now a good time?"

"Yes. Thank you." I was grateful for the disruption in the tense conversation. Zinny's neck was getting red, which meant she was getting invested in her anger.

He stepped inside and put the bags down on the chairs. "There's a bunch of stuff in here, and it's a few different sizes because I didn't know how formfitting you like your clothes."

"Tonight? I think we might be in the mood for comfy. It's been a lot." I started plucking things out of the bags.

As we were pulling things out, Leto came out of the bathroom wrapped in a towel.

Zinny snorted. "They have robes."

"Yeah, which is great, but I suck at wearing those. They come undone and then it's awkward." He stepped next to me.

Animal pointed to a small black bag. "I actually was able to grab you some things from the house. We have a lot extra for our guys."

"Thanks. Appreciate it." He grabbed the black bag and disappeared back into the bathroom.

"Dinner is in an hour if you guys are up for it. If not, there are a ton of menus in the kitchen. Just let the guys up front know to grab your delivery." Animal winked at us both as we thanked him again.

Aster said some muted words to Animal in the hallway, then appeared in the theater room. "Heard we had goodies in here to cover our goodies."

"We do. It's supposed to be baggy, so no need to poison yourself." Zinny gave Aster a scathing glare.

"You know, for someone who loves me as much as you do, you sure talk to me like you hate me." Aster folded her arms under her boobs.

Leto came out of the bathroom with his hair brushed back. He had on dark jeans and a black button-up. He could easily pass for one of Mercy's men. The black in his shirt brought out his long lashes.

Aster looked him up and down. "So he looks great in a suit *and* in casual clothes."

Zinny offered, "And rumor has it, he looks best wearing nothing at all."

Leto's ears got red with a blush.

"Sorry again for bursting in on you. Aster had the phone, and we weren't sure if you had swiped it." I shrugged as I offered my apology. I had to do what I had to do to keep us all safe.

"Your hand was forced. No worries. I can handle it." He folded the black bag his clothes had come in.

Zinny and Aster had picked out outfits, and the theater room had turned into a makeshift wardrobe. I grabbed a soft, black dress and a pair of sandals.

I walked into the bathroom but left the door open as I got into my clothes. I flipped my hair over and fluffed it out. I was exhausted both mentally and physically. My muscles were still sore from all the activity and stress. I was very interested in a few glasses of wine. The bathroom had an entire makeup kit, so I added a bit of mascara and a matte lip. That was all I had the energy for.

When I came out to the theater room, Leto had sorted the clothing and organized it by chair.

"Thanks?"

"Yeah, sorry. I'm like a compulsive neatener. I can't relax unless everything is in order." He stuck his thumbs into his pockets. "You look amazing."

"Oh. Thanks. Are you ready to walk over to the big house?" I slipped my phone into the pocket in my dress.

"Yes." He held out his arm to me like we were headed to church.

When we got to the top of the stairs, Zinny and Aster were waiting. Zinny had picked jeans and a white blouse and strappy sandals.

Aster had on a tank dress like mine, but she had paired it with Converse. "How is my stomach growling so soon after the shark coochie board?"

"A what now?" Leto held up a hand. "I thought I was hearing things before. Are you talking about a shark's...coochie?"

Zinny stepped forward. "She thinks she's funny. It's called a charcuterie board if you're fancy."

Leto sniffed and smiled a little. "It is kind of funny."

Zinny swept past him. "You would say that."

I made a face at Aster who reciprocated our silent laugh.

Leto stayed near Aster and me as we walked out of the house. There were two men standing outside. I was pretty sure they were there to watch over Leto, but I also had a suspicion maybe we weren't as trusted as I thought.

CHAPTER
EIGHTEEN

T he guards were armed to the teeth. And they were not distracted by the three gorgeous women I was going on a short walk with. Oh wait, I caught the shorter one peeking at the ladies.

I couldn't help but wonder what they had gotten out of Max. The fact that he was a prisoner here was mind-boggling. He'd been such an institution in the criminal life I was involved in. Like a god. And these ladies had just infiltrated his safe space and stole him, and freed my brother as an afterthought.

This was another level of danger and skill, and I had no idea how this ended for me. I wasn't sure how in charge these ladies were. I'd heard that Mercy was a standup guy, but there was a lot of folklore on the street. Not all of it could be taken as gospel.

When we got to the main house, one of the guards opened the door. The dining room was just off a mud room. The thick chunky table could easily seat twelve. The matching chairs had to be made up of half a tree apiece. Music was playing and Animal was pouring wine.

Zinny made a beeline for him and her attitude instantly changed. Instead of sulking about her fight with the other girls, she was radiant. T was there, and a few other guys from the job that brought me in.

It was not fancy. They had the table filled with all different taco supplies, and everyone was encouraged to take a plate.

I stayed close to Indy. She looked tired to me. I hadn't known her that long, but the spark that I saw in the casino was definitely more dull.

"You want me to get you a glass?" I tipped my head in Animal's direction.

"Sure. That would be great, thanks." She grabbed a plate and started adding taco shells.

When I was near Animal, he put down the wine.

"Can I grab a glass of red for Indy and Aster?"

Animal nodded at me. "Go right ahead."

He literally towered over me. His deep voice seemed to settle the whole room down. He was a whole mood. "How's it going?"

"Well, fantastic being that I spent part of my day in a coffin." I toasted the two wine glasses together.

"That's a great way to look at probably every day you've got left on this planet." He put his hand on my shoulder. "Excuse me."

He moved in the direction of the kitchen. I found Indy and Aster and handed them each a glass of wine. They had picked seats next to each other at the table. I put the glass down and they smiled and took a sip at the same time.

I headed back to get my own drink when another guy came up next to me. He was the driver from when Indy and I had fallen asleep together. "Hey, buddy." He clapped me on the back. "Don't be tryin' to case the joint. It's not worth it and we're already prepared to blow your balls off."

I nodded like he'd told me his aunt made a great pie for the county fair. "Noted. For sure. Honestly, I'm just happy to be here. I won't ever even remember that I was." I grabbed a beer and tried to seem as passive as possible.

A stunning girl with rainbow hair came by. "Try to leave the new people alone. Geeze."

The man that had threatened me slipped his arm around Rainbow Girl's shoulders. She held out her hand. "I'm Ember, Nix's sister. And this is Sherlock, my boyfriend. Nice to meet you. Cool that you got to work with the Lady Mafia. I've been obsessed with them since I learned who they were."

"Nice to meet you. And I met your boyfriend briefly in a car. I feel like I've been a little obsessed with them, too. They're great at what they do." Like this was a normal party and this was a normal discussion. What these women were good at was not something that would normally bring much praise.

Ember threaded her fingers through Lock's. "I mean, they could almost be superheroes. It would be great to have more role models for girls."

"Yeah. Except for all the murder." I shrugged my shoulders, and I felt like I was failing at small talk.

Ember tilted her head. "Actually, there were zero fatalities today, so that makes what they do even more impressive."

Nix came up next to Lock and Ember. "You maybe need to go find something else to do."

Lock took the cue even though Ember made a disappointed noise and started to maneuver her away from me. Nix pointed to the kitchen. "Your niece is in there."

The sheer mention of the niece wiped away any disappointment Ember had. I followed the line of sight to see a beautiful woman holding a plump baby. Ember beelined it to be close to her.

Nix stepped next to me when Ember and Lock left.

"You're looking at my kid," he offered.

"She's adorable. Congratulations." I went to step past him, but thought better of it and went to take a sip of my beer.

"Now that you've laid eyes on my kid, part of you will always belong to me." He looked down his nose at me.

I paused my beer midway to my mouth. I wasn't sure what he meant or how I was supposed to respond.

"Act accordingly." He left me to join his daughter and sister in the kitchen.

My appetite for tacos went down the drain. This seemed like a lovely dinner party, but I had to keep it all in focus. This man and the people he surrounded himself with were the best of the best. And somewhere in this building Max was either alive or dead, having had his fate doled out.

I finished drinking my beer, but I didn't taste it on the way down. I was in a den of vipers. They were pretty and clearly loved each other, but they were murderers just the same. I wondered where my brother was. I wondered if I was getting out of this alive. And then I thought better of it and grabbed two more beers. I was going to wash this night away. I had no other choice.

CHAPTER
NINETEEN

Eventually, we all retired to the firepit area outside. There were benches, nice Adirondack chairs, and a few rocking chairs. The stars were out, crisp and clear. Leto had gotten quiet after Animal, Lock, Ember, and Nix spoke to him. I didn't know what they said, but he had taken to drinking exclusively afterward. He didn't try any food. Ember had made a point of making sure her favorite new playlist was piped in on the speakers in the backyard.

It would be a cozy evening with any other crew. I was under no illusions. This was a dangerous group. We had very similar goals, and for that, we all respected each other. But he had many, many enemies. Most kept their distance out of fear, but it didn't mean my girls and I wouldn't get caught in the crossfire somewhere. I stopped drinking wine after two glasses. I was tired, and the alcohol was making that worse. I knew I'd sleep like the dead in the guest house. It was well guarded, and barring anyone moving on Nix and company while we visited, it should all be pretty simple.

I stood to find the bathroom, and T walked up next to me.

"Let's go together." She was not the kind of lady that did group restroom trips, so I knew something was up. She walked me through a few hallways, and then she showed me to her and Animal's private wing. After using the facilities, I met her back in the sitting room. She was perched on the arm of a chair with a remote in her hand.

I perched on the other chair. "What's up?"

She sighed. "I feel like there's no good way to tell you this, other than let you see it for yourself."

She pointed the remote at the TV and hit play.

Max was sitting in a chair and he looked fine. Wet and tired, but fine. I had expected to see more remnants of how, exactly, Mercy's people got him to talk.

"We don't leave marks," T offered as if she knew what I had been preparing myself for.

Max leveled a stare just right of the camera. "The place we keep the new employees is very full at the moment. And very hard to get to."

A man stepped closer to Max, who instantly leaned in the opposite direction.

T pointed to the man. "It was his sister that was trafficked."

I nodded. I'd agreed to get Max for Mercy on that information alone. Seeing the brother in the same room with Max made me feel like the job had been well worth it.

"They're not employees, I'm sorry. Just habit. Habit. Nothing more. They're victims. But you have to know, I'm not in charge of it all. We all report to someone, right? My boss has a taste for this type of thing." Max hung his head.

T paused the video. "I'm not trying to convince you. I just wanted you to know that this isn't finished yet. Professional courtesy. A lot of these girls are runaways or their placement didn't work out. Also, Mercy told me that your identity might have been compromised, but Zinny and Aster are in the clear, as far as we can tell."

"Let me talk to Aster and Zinny." I folded my arms under my boobs. We were all having trouble getting along, but freeing a bunch of girls would be very hard to walk away from.

That evening, Zinny, Aster, and I all sat in the living room. Leto was in his bedroom downstairs. We had guards placed outside, but T had assured me that we were free to come and go as we pleased.

"Do they know how many?" Zinny squinted at a spot above my head.

"It's fluid. Girls are in and out quickly. They are trapped, caught, replaced, and then sent out." I tapped my fingers on my leg. "But it has the sound of a camp. Prisoners. A commodity."

Aster had her head resting on the back of the couch. "You know we have to do it."

"There will always be reasons to stay. Revenge to be had. Things will be presented to us time and time again." I was playing devil's advocate. I knew my girls. They would want this.

Zinny had a hollow laugh. "Don't feed us that shit, Indy. We all know how it's going to go down."

I sank back into my seat. She was right. I wasn't going to be able to sleep again if I didn't at least try to put an end to this one.

When we were teens, Zinny, Aster, and I were swindled. We were convinced that we could make great money taking a few pictures and spending time with some businessmen.

Tron was a scumbag, but he could talk a good game, especially to sixteen-year-old girls. We thought his fancy car was a big deal. We thought his pile of cash was endless.

Zinny and I didn't listen to Aster when she said her gut was telling her no. That there was something not right with Tron.

And looking back, both Zinny and I knew it, too. The rush of danger made us feel something—like we were adults. Like we were tough.

Tron had picked us up from school. Halfway to our first party with him, Aster hopped out of the car. We stayed and she fled.

Later that night, when Zinny and I were huddled together, very, very far over our heads, it was Aster that burst into the house with an entire football team.

There were cheerleaders, and a band as well. Instead of a

shoot-out, they pretty much pep rallied us out of the building. We knew from that point on we had to listen to Aster's gut. It was her gift.

I knew what we were going to do. "Yeah. We're in until they are all out." I stood up and stretched. It was time to get some sleep.

"What are you going to do about your pet?" Aster pointed toward Leto's bedroom.

"I don't honestly know. He kidnapped me first, so." I turned to Zinny and Aster. "This job will be the most difficult ever. You two have to be on the same page. If we aren't in sync, it can be deadly. And not just for us." I didn't need to say more. I knew they were picturing the girls we were headed in to save.

I closed my bedroom door and was quietly relieved. I talked a big game, but I wasn't ready for the Lady Mafia to be dead and buried. I wanted us to go out with a serious world-changing bang.

CHAPTER

TWENTY

I heard the bedroom door down the hall close and feet headed up the stairs. The Lady Mafia had had a meeting in the living room while I lay on my back in a fancy bed.

After a few beats of silence, there was a light knock on my door. I hopped off the bed and swung it open. I had on a pair of black sweats and that was it.

Indy was holding her phone out. "Before I go to bed, I wanted to offer you a chance to tell your brother that you're okay."

I stepped backward into the bedroom so she could come inside.

She was soft with no makeup, and I had a flash of a future with her. Laughing while painting a bedroom in our first house, raking leaves together, sitting in a school auditorium cheering on our kids' holiday play.

I took a sharp intake of breath. I'd never had my future life flash before my eyes so completely.

Her beautiful eyes looked at me quizzically. "You okay?"

I bit the insides of my cheeks. "I'm good. And yes, I'd love to tell Matt I'm alive, but aren't you concerned someone will track your phone?"

She set the phone on the nightstand and sat on my bed. "Do you think I would ever use a phone that could be tracked?"

She tilted her head like she was amazed at my shortsightedness.

I ran a hand down my face. "Right. Not your first rodeo."

She picked up the phone again. "Let me set it up, and then you can ring through. Say anything stupid and I will slice something off your body." After she pressed a few buttons, she held it out. "And keep it on speaker."

"Great. Great plan." I took the phone and dialed my brother's number. I was far past thinking these people didn't already have all his information. Mercy and this Lady Mafia were like 007 level pros.

I set the phone to speaker and held it just in front of my mouth. My brother's voice was on the phone, obviously hesitant to pick up what had to be an unknown number. "Yeah?"

"Yeah, bro, it's me. I'm alive and shit." I sat down next to Indy. Her whole body bounced a little with my added weight on the mattress.

"Tell me the name of my pet turtle." Matt was scared this was a trick, and that was fair.

"Turdie. It was a horrible name and you were a stupid kid." I laughed a little at the end, thinking of him standing in his underwear declaring the turtle his gift from the backyard. I had tried to talk him out of the name, but he was dead set on it.

"I was a dumb shit. I'm so glad you're alive." Matt's relieved exhale sounded like a wind tunnel through the speaker.

"Are you still alive?" I asked. I had no idea what had possibly happened to him when he went with the guys.

"I am. I'd like to say I'm a borderline hostage at this point? Bitz said that he's hanging on to me until you pay him and the crew for the work they did for you." Matt sounded tired.

"Funny thing, I'm a borderline hostage, too."

Indy sucked on her teeth. I didn't have to look at her to know that she was giving me a warning to watch what I said.

"That's unfortunate. How do we get you ransomed so you can get me ransomed?"

Indy grabbed the pen and pad of paper from inside the nightstand drawer. She jotted down her terms.

You have to help us on the job. Do a good job and we will pay you.

I covered the speaker. "How long?"

"A few weeks," she mouthed.

"Matt, are they going to be cool to you for a few weeks? I've got to get some shit together." I bit my lip and listened.

"Yeah. I'm teaching them how to count cards and bet horses, so as long as I keep giving them useful stuff, I should be good."

"Okay. Sounds like a plan. Stay safe. Stay out of trouble. Love you, man." I ended the call and handed the phone to Indy. "Thanks. You didn't have to do that."

"I'm a sucker for siblings, and he seemed pretty attached to you when he and I were in the hot tub together." She twirled the phone in her hands.

"You were in a hot tub with my brother?" As far as I knew, he was Max's prisoner.

"Oh yeah. He was set up sweet at the casino. In-room hot tub, awesome food, liquor, and a TV." She stood from my bed.

"So glad I risked my life to save him from that horrible torture." I stood as well, a little too soon. I almost collided with her. I had to put my arms around her to keep us both from falling.

She put one of her hands against my bare chest and gasped as I pulled her hard to me.

"Sorry. Damn. Sorry. I should've waited a second."

She looked up at me with her terracotta eyes. My whole body was on alert. We were just a few mistakes away from finding out what turned each other on.

"Matt was in danger. You were right to want to get him out.

106

Max is unstable and unpredictable." She wasn't pulling out of my arms, so I kept them around her.

"Is Max still in the present? Or should you be saying he *was* unstable?" I watched her look from my chest to my mouth. She gently played with my chest hair.

God, she was beautiful.

"I don't know, and I didn't ask. My guess is, he'll be alive until we finish this last job. Just in case we need any information or leverage. But how Mercy does his business is just that—his business." Her tongue peeked out.

"That makes sense." I was just stalling now, to keep her in my arms.

"Yeah, perfect sense." She leaned forward a bit and I leaned down. Our lips almost touched.

We were so close to a kiss, all we had to do was...

She took a step backward. "Goodnight, Leto."

I let my hands fall to my sides and closed my eyes. "Goodnight, Indy. My door is open, if..."

When I opened my eyes, she was gone. Silent. My door was ajar and I could still smell her conditioner. I looked down at my alert penis.

"Sorry, dude. That one's going to hurt." My balls tried to crawl inside my body as I anticipated an epic case of lover's nuts.

The dream I was having of Indy was pornographic, down to the cheesy music. My blue balls had certainly tucked me in last night. I woke up to a hand gently touching my face, skimming my five o'clock shadow. Then a gentle lick. I turned my face and then the panting turned the dream of Indy into a werewolf person. I opened my eyes to a slimy pink tongue. It slapped across my face in a thorough lick. The toxic breath made me gag.

I pushed an adorable, excited Labrador retriever off of my bed. I used my sheets to wipe my face.

I submitted to the energetic, immediate friendship that the dog offered. There was a low whistle somewhere in the distance and the dog stopped, stood stock still and then took off. The only remnants of were was a smattering of dog hair.

After I used the bathroom and got dressed in Mercy crew-like clothes, I headed upstairs to the smell of coffee.

The three Lady Mafia and T were all holding coffee cups. The discussion that had been murmuring between them was instantly paused.

I met Indy's gaze and she took a sip of her coffee cup, the curve of the mug matching the one on her lips.

"Uh. Good morning?" I heard a tail thumping before the Lab I had recently wrestled with came out from under the table. As I reached down to pet his excited body, he swung his snoot hard toward my crotch.

"Whoa, dude. We don't know each other like that yet." The Lab licked my hands, my shirt, and some of the air around both.

"Bacon!" T snapped her fingers and Bacon, the dog, responded quickly. He gave her a look that expressed deep apologies before snapping to his happy-go-lucky resting face.

"That dog's name is Bacon?" I hadn't heard of that name on a dog before.

T nodded. "Yeah. An asshole was going to kill him for stealing his bacon."

Aster held out her mug. "I'm willing to bet that Bacon got all of the bacon that guy ever had on his plate."

T touched her mug to Aster's. "You would be correct."

Indy pushed away from the table and came close to me. "Bagels are over there and there's a fresh pot of coffee."

I turned to find the setup on the counter near the giant fridge. While I prepped my breakfast, Indy watched me. All of a sudden my fingers seemed to be foreign to me. She made me nervous. I smeared cream cheese onto my bagel like a two-year-old.

As if he was magic, Bacon was underfoot immediately, his tongue lolling out and dripping a bit on my boot. "Is he allowed to have people food now? I mean, I know the story and all, but some dogs have adverse reactions to some stuff."

"He's sort of been a wireless vacuum this morning. And everyone is required to give him the last bite of their food. Seems like a tradition and a rule," Indy offered.

"Understood. Last bite for Bacon." I set my plate down and went to the sink, cleaning the cream cheese from my hands.

Indy handed me a napkin. "Come sit, we're making some plans."

I walked over, carefully navigating a focused Bacon as he weaved in and out of my legs. When I sat, Bacon rested his head on my knee.

Indy started to lay things out for me after she took her seat.

"Max has provided a detailed blueprint of the buildings as far as he knows, but Animal thinks there is still some stuff he isn't telling us."

"We need a set of inside eyes." Zinny rubbed her temples.

"I disagree." Indy shook her head. "This is a place that we need to be very cautious of. I'm not willing to have you guys in there." Indy's eyes flashed.

They were butting heads again. I quietly munched on my bagel and petted Bacon's head.

"You know and I know that the men in charge don't know everything. We're talking innocent lives," Zinny offered.

We waited while Indy ruminated. "As far as I'm concerned, you and Aster are innocent, too."

Zinny burst out laughing and even Aster started to smile.

"Baby, please don't call me innocent this early in the morning. Damn." Zinny slapped her hand on the table for emphasis.

Indy was not amused. "Tell me again how you want to make it work."

Aster scooted forward in her chair. "We know they comb the parking lots for new girls. Zinny and I can make it look like our car broke down once we know where they're fishing for girls. And if we don't get taken, then we can do it the old-fashioned way."

"What if you're made?" Indy rubbed her thumb on the mug's handle.

Aster reached over and grabbed the coffee carafe to refill her drink.

"I would need a lot of reassurance that I could contact you guys. A lot." Indy was softening to the idea, so it would seem.

"It's going to be dangerous, Indy. It's what we do. Why are we so gun-shy all of a sudden?" Aster put a heap of cream in her drink.

Indy tucked her hair behind her ear. "I feel like we are pressing fate on this one. Like we're pushing for a fight."

"So we just leave those ladies in that place? To face God knows what?" Zinny stood and walked away from the table.

Indy tilted her head to one side and then another. "You know that's not it. I just like to have all the problems and plans and contingencies worked out."

"You can do that while we're on the inside." Zinny pulled her hair into a ponytail while she talked.

Indy nodded slowly. She didn't seem convinced. I handed my last bite of bagel to Bacon who inhaled it.

T stood and Bacon went to her side. "I think I'll visit Max and get a little more information my way. Then I can give you guys my opinion and you can take it or leave it."

Bacon followed T after giving everyone around the table a nose boop.

Indy stood as well. "I think we've done all we can until we hear back." She turned to me. "I'm headed out to get some air, you want to come?"

I picked up my plate and a few others on the table. "Sure." I put the plates into the sink and hustled to keep up with her.

As I turned to close the door behind me, I watched as Zinny's tough exterior cracked and her shoulders slumped.

CHAPTER
TWENTY-ONE

"Hey, is it cool if we go for a walk?" I asked the guard by the door. I knew I was allowed to come and go, but I wasn't sure what everyone's comfort level with Leto was.

"Are you packing?" he asked as if it was a question about the weather.

"Yeah." I never went anywhere without something that would give me an edge if I needed it.

"Then you're cool to walk." He sat back down on the chair on the porch.

Leto ducked out from behind me and waited.

I looked around at the sprawling compound. The sheets of gray rock made a path that led to a parting of tall hedges. I headed in that direction.

Leto kept a few feet between us. We walked for a few minutes before he spoke, "You've got some tension back there."

I shot him a look. "You're an expert on us already?"

"No. Not even a little, but I've followed the legend of you ladies for a while. I researched some of the jobs they know you did. You're tight. Like siblings who love each other tight." He kicked a lone rock off the path. "And I'm like that with my dumbass brother."

"We didn't do half the jobs that are rumored to be ours." I wasn't keen on opening up to Leto just yet.

"Yeah. You ladies have a fingerprint. In and out. Clean. That last one was not clean." He stuck his hands in his pockets, curving his massive shoulders inward.

"No, it wasn't. It was messy. But we knew getting to Max would be. He's so well guarded." I stopped and took in what was beyond the hedges.

There was a huge pool, a fountain in the center. Every side had steps leading into it. There were massive statues and a few benches. I headed in the direction of the benches.

"Well, if it's any consolation, my planned event went sideways, too." He ruffled his hair and shot me a rueful glance.

"I bet it did. It was a classic screw-up." I started picturing how our antics would come off in a retelling between others in the criminal world.

Leto's face lit up. "Oh. Now you're picturing it, right? The shrimp girl screaming her orgasms? The most inept group of fighting women turning the tables and just pantsing the entire operation? Yeah, I feel like a mastermind."

"And now you're technically kidnapped," I added.

"Yup, I'm never working in this business again." He gestured to the bench and I sat down.

He took a seat next to me. "You were worried about your brother and took on one of the toughest assignments ever. We don't do our best work when family is involved."

"Thanks. Tell that to everyone else. But thanks for getting Matt. Did I say that yet?" He turned to face me and he swept his gaze over my face and back to my eyes.

"You're welcome." I focused on the water in the pool. It glinted in tiny waves in the sun.

"You didn't have to do that." He put his hand over mine on the bench.

I gave him a skeptical look. "Are you hitting on me?"

He pulled his hand away. "No. No. Shit. Sorry, I was going for sincere. Not creepy. Sorry. You're really beautiful, I bet everything I do will come off as a flirt."

He held his hands up like I had my gun aimed at him.

I rolled my eyes and ran my tongue over my teeth.

"What are your concerns for Zinny and Aster with this next job? From one shit show runner to another." He tapped his feet.

"I mean, aside from all the normal things? Getting killed, getting caught, retaliation from other angry people?" I ran my thumb on my cuticle.

"Yes, aside from that."

"We don't know how many girls there are. Moving one person is hard enough. Moving ten? Moving fifty? It takes weeks to prepare for a bus trip for retirees for that amount of people. Never mind sneaking them out of basically an untraceable prison." I took a deep breath.

"Okay, agreed. But won't you have better intel if Aster and Zinny are on this inside?" He leaned toward me.

"At what cost? If I wasn't made, it could have been me on the inside and them on the outside." I covered my eyes from the sun and looked at him.

"What's your end goal? For all this. I mean, I assume you have all the money you could want. What's driving you?" He parted his lips.

"Yeah. That's the glaring problem. I don't think any of us thought about the way this would end."

I was startled when I heard Zinny clear her throat. She stepped up into the pool surround with Aster on her side. "I think we didn't expect to survive."

Zinny and Aster came to stand in front of Leto and me. Zinny put her hands on her hips.

"T got back to us. There are at least thirty girls."

And that was the challenge laid out in front of me. Thirty was so many. Too many.

I stood. "If we weren't built to do this exact thing, then I don't know why we were put on this earth. If we don't chop the head off this snake, more girls will be taken. We have to destroy and demoralize them so that no one else wants to do this." I walked into my girls and we hugged it out. "Let's go."

It was clear what I was afraid of, but I was afraid of doing nothing to save these girls more.

CHAPTER
TWENTY-TWO

Once they had made the decision, the Lady Mafia was in full swing. I wasn't sure what my role here was. Indy asked my opinion from time to time, but mostly, I think I was eye candy.

I didn't know there were people like these ladies. Doing the wrong thing to get the right result.

The systematic way Max was used to shape the plans to attack this island—and we knew now it was surrounded by water—was equal parts effective as it was terrifying. It made me realize that I had worked on the outskirts of the criminal world, but these guys? They could teach master's level courses on how best to use a human asset.

T would arrive with blueprints or names. Sometimes she had a Google search that led to a missing poster. The extent of the danger and damage was filling out. They say knowledge is power, but the more we found out about this place? Knowledge was anger. Like the pieces of a puzzle—the edges and corners forming. The girls there were sometimes trafficked, sometimes used to breed—all sorts of horrors.

Watching Indy's eyes get more and more determined was a lesson in the force of a woman. They narrowed down the habits and paths the crew that worked there followed. Learning about the island was the main focus of everyday. Aster, Zinny, and Indy also worked out, took target practice time, and stretched on the regular. They gave themselves two weeks to prepare to have Indy and Zinny caught. They were antsy.

INDY and I were in the theater room with one day to go before Indy and Zinny started fishing for getting picked up. She had her feet up and her hair in a towel.

"I hear your brother is doing well." Indy had a bottle of moisturizer and squirted some of the cream onto her hands.

"That's good. He has uses. Unfortunately, he also has demons." I rested my hands behind my neck.

"Has he always been like that?" She started rubbing her elbow.

"Sort of. He's always been a risk taker. He's jumped off the roof of our family home like four times and he broke a bone each time. He doesn't learn—even when he's already experienced pain as a result." I could still see him, one hundred miles an hour past the window. The horrible noise of something cracking while his body hit the yard.

"What do you like about him?" Indy was in an inquisitive mood. Maybe distracting herself from wanting to move on the island before they were completely ready.

"I like his ballsiness. I like his complete lack of self-awareness and the fact that he thinks he can kick everyone's ass. And he can't. He's successfully kicked his own ass many times." I put my hands on my lap. "You know, he always makes me laugh. I'm not sure if siblings have some sort of inside road to humor, but I think he's hilarious. Plus, he is my brother. He's my responsibility." I shrugged.

"Is he now? Aren't you guys full size grownups? Like, I think his choices are his." She set the lotion down on the ground.

"Maybe so. I just can't turn my back on him. I promised my dad on his deathbed that I would look out for Matt, and I don't break promises. Even if no one would blame me for doing it." I could still smell the hospital disinfectant when I thought of my dad. It was a core memory. Something that was both real and unreal at the same time. At seventeen, I was in charge of not only myself, but my brother.

"Sorry to hear about your dad." Indy touched my wrist gently.

"Thanks. He was a good guy—just couldn't beat cancer. I'll tell you what, my brother is the spitting image of my dad. They look like time travelers in the pictures we have of them together."

"What about your mom? Was she in any pictures?"

I liked that she still had her hand on my hand. "Nah. Mom left dad soon after Matt was born. Dad said she had to find herself, but the rumor mill around town was that she had two guys she was living with. It's where my sisters came from. Just brutal ammunition to give other kids growing up. The amount of 'jokes' I heard about my mom and her way of life was enough to last a lifetime. When I saw her it was always at restaurants and sometimes court rooms. After dad died, she was more involved."

"Oh, that's too much. Kids can be such assholes." She nodded.

"Were they assholes to you? Or were you the asshole?"

She took her hand away and I wished I had worded it differently.

"I think a little bit of both. I had a chip on my shoulder when I entered foster care. My mom had given me to my grandmother, who then decided I was too much. And then came the foster care hopping. One to the other to the other. Until I was in the one with Zinny and Aster. That one was different. The foster parents were like—I don't know—called to be around kids. They were super invested in all of our upbringing and school." She stood.

"They saved our lives, I think. They trusted us, and that was unique. They specialized in older kids, and those kids had some shit pasts. Like the trafficking we are invested in putting a stop to. Some of our foster siblings would come to the home after being in a situation like that. Hell, Zinny was kidnapped for a short time. It was like evil knew where to find the defenseless. You know?"

She paced. "Bill, our foster dad, he wanted us to be able to stand up for ourselves. He was a black belt in a few different disciplines, and no girl left his house without being able to flip him over their back and incapacitate him. I swear, he had a bad back from the sheer amount of times it hit the ground."

"Bill and Kelly. They were good ones. They still are good ones. They restored our faith in some of humanity. And Aster, Zinny, and I decided we were the best family we were going to get, so we made a pact to stick together."

"Was it like that the whole time? Since then until now?" That had to be ten years. Maybe more.

"Yeah. That's what happened, but we can't do this forever. You know how physical it is. How much we ask of our bodies every time. How much we ask of our minds."

I shook my head. "I'm not sure I know how much it takes from you ladies. You're on another level. Explains why Max wanted you so bad. You're dangerous."

Her mouth turned up a little at the corners before she winked. "Speaking of which, the girls and I have a session."

I wasn't sure what a session included, but I knew I wasn't invited. I held out my hand to her and she took it to pull herself up. I felt the heat between the two of us as we got closer. One leg slipped out of her robe as she turned to walk away.

Creamy. Her skin was creamy, and I felt like an old-ass creeper saying the word in my head. I could spend an entire evening with her thighs wrapped around my head. I hoped it happened. Maybe tonight.

CHAPTER
TWENTY-THREE

S ession time was necessary. It was how Bill taught us once we were able to perform to his expected level.

Aster and Z were already dressed. I took my spot after twirling my mostly dry hair into a bun.

A triangle. We waited until we were ready, making eye contact. There was no need for a starting pistol or a green light. We all felt the energy shift and change.

It was time to fight. We were the best we knew at what we did. To keep ourselves sharp, we attacked.

This wasn't drunken shenanigans. This was pressing each other as hard as we could and more so we wouldn't lose any skills. I tried to kill my two best friends, and they tried to kill me back.

Sometimes we brought weapons; sometimes we didn't. No rules. They would team up on me at times, and then we would switch out. Each of us took swings, blocked hits, and disarmed each other. After a good thirty-minute session, the energy would change again. It was over. Like the end of a thunderstorm, the clearing in our eyes and our demeanors brought relief.

We met in the center, sweating, limping a bit. I wrapped my hand around the back of their necks as we all touched foreheads. We'd done it on our own. Aster had had a particularly tough session with Bill and was thinking of bailing. Instead, I told her we would be like lionesses and bump heads and stay together. It was something silly at fourteen, but it had stuck.

As we walked out of the gym that Nix had on the property, Aster pulled out her phone from her drawstring bag. "He's trying again."

She held up the screen and we watched as Spenser struggled under the weight of a large flower arrangement on Aster's doorbell cam.

"Look how hard he's trying."

Z snorted. "Those are lilies and they make you sneeze fart."

Aster frowned before flicking the video away.

I put my arm through hers. "We have people to kill and girls to save. Spenser would literally crap himself if he knew what you're up to."

Aster tucked her phone away, but I saw the ghost of what she hoped would have been her future locked in her faraway gaze.

Aster wanted a tire swing and a sprinkler out front. She wanted one of those fake benches so that the Amazon man could hide her packages for her sticky toddlers.

Spenser could have been any man. Aster really didn't care who was cast in the role of her husband.

When we got back to the guest house, we divided so we could shower. Z caught my eye and we said nothing, but I knew she had noticed the same thing that I had. Aster wasn't going to marry Spenser, we wouldn't allow that, but Z and I would have to let her go someday. Someday soon.

I shook out the worries of our future and went over the plans again as I let the hot water rewet my hair. It was sweaty business, kicking ass. And preparing to kick ass. There was something lingering like an aftertaste in my intuition. I wasn't sure what it was, but I didn't like it. I must have been in the shower longer than I thought because I heard Leto give a gentle knock on the door.

"You alright in there?"

I looked down at my sudsy body. There was one sure way to feel better, and I knew Leto would be down for it.

"Yeah. Can you come in?" I watched him enter the bathroom from the glass surround. The steam made him blurry, but I didn't miss his hopeful and excited gaze.

Leto was a great looking guy. I was used to that in this field. Dangerous guys, deadly guys. Something about his devotion to his brother spoke to me in a way that made me want to trust him.

"You in the mood?" I wiped the steam away from the shower glass, giving him a full view.

"Anytime. Every time."

Leto ripped off his shirt but stepped into the shower with his jeans on, like I was on fire and he had to save me. I laughed as he grabbed me.

"Slippery, sexy baby. Finally." Leto traced a hand over my body, then greedily used both hands. "So much good stuff to see."

He was making me laugh with his urgency.

He used the flat of his hand to run over the colors of my elaborate tattoo. I let my head tilt back when he felt between my legs. The spray from the rainforest showerhead pounded on my face.

"Yeah. Put your head back. Yes." Leto stopped moving. "We're cool to have crazy sex, right?"

I stepped out of the steam and wiped the water off of my face. "It better be crazy. I want clown shoes and flame throwers."

"I'll honk like a donkey, whatever you need. Just touch my dick. Please." Leto started working on his pants. They were getting somehow bigger and tighter as the denim soaked through.

He started to panic. "Oh God, my pants! They are permanent pants. My dick is in prison. I hate jeans."

I waited for a few seconds before reaching into his pocket. He had a pocketknife there and I flipped the blade open.

He put his chin to the side and gave me a wide-eyed stare. "Changed my mind about the dick. I was kidding. I don't even have a dick. I'm like a Ken doll."

"I've seen your giant dick before, remember?" I grabbed the

waistband of his pants and pulled out a little slack. He closed his eyes and held his breath as I hacked through the denim. I was careful not to cut him, but I did let my nails scrape a little just to keep him on edge.

Eventually, he was wearing only a pair of denim knee-highs.

I closed the blade and set it on the shower shelf. He popped open one eye. "Wow. This is a lewk."

He was trying to be funny, but his ridiculous member was taking up all the space. His eyes softened and then darkened. He was completely erect, waiting. The water was dripping off the edge of his nose and his jaw. I got to see a few tattoos that were new to me.

"So are we just gonna stand around? All three of us?" I motioned to his dick.

"Nah." He took two quick steps toward me and put his hand to my neck. He pinned me to the marble wall and looked down at me. "I've always been delicate with ladies, but I'm thinking you can handle it rough."

I wrapped both my hands around him. "That's true. Go as hard as you want. If I don't like it? You'll know."

Leto tipped his head back and roared into the water stream. He let go of my neck and tossed me over his shoulder. "Got to get this soap off of you."

Between spanks and caresses, Leto made sure I was clean, using the handheld showerhead to get between my legs while biting at my thigh.

I could reach his dick, and almost get it in my mouth. He was really so big it was almost a problem. Almost.

"Let's go." He turned off the water and grabbed a towel on his way out the door. He covered my bottom with it. We were lucky that no one else was in the house, but I was grateful none of the guards outside would see me for all I was worth if they looked in the window at that moment.

After the door was closed to my room, he set me down on the

bed. "I've pictured this so many times. How is it better? How are you better than my filthy imagination?"

I slipped a hand between my legs and started to rub.

"Oh, hell no. That's for me." Leto bent at the waist, first going from one breast to the other, licking and sucking. His hand was circling me, feeling my inner thighs.

I grabbed his leg and pulled him to stand over me. His dick was mine. I started on him immediately. It was too much, he was too much, but I tried. I got him down as far as I could.

When I took a breath, he grabbed my hips and pulled me more onto the bed so his knees could go on either side of my head.

While I occupied myself with him, I felt his flat tongue right where I needed it. Just when I was ready to slam my legs shut from the sensations, he pried them open. He knew everything about me then. He could see anything he wanted. I slid his dick down between my breasts, rubbing him with them so I could get some friction to his shaft. He raised his hips and spoke between my legs, but I couldn't hear him.

His toned abs quivered when I sucked in one of his testicles and used my tongue to explore that tender area. Then I was back to the tip, circling with my tongue before sucking as hard as I could.

His fingers slid inside me and his tongue was flicking so fast I couldn't think.

I started to come, my legs shaking as he slid in another finger. He pulled away and got between my legs. "I have to see this. Come."

He sat up and used one hand on my clit, the other pumping away.

"Say my name, baby. Say it."

"Leto." I could barely gasp it out, and all I could see was white.

I felt his mouth on me again, sucking on my clit, moving his fingers in a way that made me leave my body.

His groping hand grabbed my breast and his jaw held me down when I tried to buck against him.

"You ready?"

Ready? I was done. I was so done. I heard a wrapper crinkle and popped open an eye to see him rolling on a condom.

Leto came to me and climbed on top. He grabbed one of my legs and put it on his shoulder. I felt a massive amount of lube being rubbed between my legs. Every time his fingers grazed my clit, I jumped like it was a hot wire.

"I'm going to go slow. Don't be a hero. When it stops, it stops."

Oh my God, he was talking about his giant salami dick. "Are you life coaching me to accept your penis?"

"You're gonna need it." He gave me a small shrug.

Then we began. He started rubbing my clit again, who came back from the dead.

When he entered me, I started to laugh. He was so big, but he knew what he was doing.

"Open your hips, Indy. Let me in." His dick was so big we both had to focus. It was an extreme sport.

I shifted my hips and tried to relax my muscles.

I watched as he stared between our legs, like he was backing a semi-truck into an ant hill.

And then I got competitive. Competitive with all the other girls that had to tell him to stop. I lifted my hips to take him faster, getting him all the way in. His eyes went wide.

"You goddamn miracle."

"Welcome. You fit. Go for it." I circled my hips for him and had the pleasure of watching his eyes roll into his head.

Leto unleashed what seemed like a lifetime of wanting and waiting. When I matched him, thrust for thrust and grabbed my breasts, he screamed like he was falling off a cliff. Then I hit him with the Kegel muscles.

He came and came, letting go of my leg so he could collapse

on top of me. I hugged him to my chest. I had feelings for this man, and it would probably be a problem.

INDY

I was armed. I had four duffle bags of every weapon and tool I could possibly think of to help us. Z and Aster were due to get involved in a dicey situation in a run-down mall. Z dressed young and Aster swallowed some shrimp.

I didn't like the idea of it. I never liked the idea, but this time it wasn't for Spenser or to fill out her favorite dress. It was to ensure that she got taken.

She even had devised shrimp pills to take with her. Little dehydrated bits of shrimp lodged in sugar pills so she could keep up the act for some time if she had to. Aster also had travel-size Epi pens. All of it was off-label stuff that Animal was able to acquire.

I was in a broken down looking van and I had brought Leto with me. We were both intent on the audio-video feed that van's camera was picking up.

"Does that look like Meatball to you?" I tapped my index finger against the screen. The beefy guy was busy buttoning and unbuttoning a vest over and over. It was ill-fitting and he couldn't get it to lay the way he wanted it to.

"I think so. I mean, the nickname would fit. He totally looks like a Meatball." Leto leaned forward a bit. "They seem like they are flanking Aster and Z—trying to distract them."

He was right. This group had done this act before over and over again.

Meatball ran up to the girls with a smile. "So sorry to bother you, but my car just ran out of gas. I was wondering if you could give me a ride?"

He was really milking the whole puppy dog eye thing. The girls bounced the idea of taking Meatball in their car. Well, the car that Nix had provided for us to use, saying it could never be traced.

And then they all moved. One after another. Leto had to put out his arm to stop me. I hadn't even realized I had headed for the doors. It was like trying to tame a wildfire with a teaspoon of water. Seeing my girls getting taken caused a vicious, spontaneous reaction inside of me.

I let Leto guide me back to my spot. I knew Aster could take down at least three of the guys surrounding her, but she let herself go rigid and her eyes go wide. Of course, this was the plan.

Zinny did the same, but when Aster stumbled and fell, Zinny's reflex was to free herself to help her.

She did it easily. Too easily.

The men that had been gathering her stepped away. I watched as the realization that she'd fucked up reached her face. The change was infinitesimal, but I knew her. Aster didn't drop her act for a second, even when they took only her in the white van that had pulled up.

I stood again, grabbing my weapons. I watched Z on the screen. She wasn't stopping them. She wasn't launching an attack. I held my stance, my guns, and my breath.

Leto leaned forward, closer to the screen.

And then the van tore off. I was out the back doors and met Z halfway.

"She waved me off." Z already knew the conversation we were going to have.

"Shit. Why?" It made no sense for Aster to go it alone. Because of her shrimp allergy, she was the most vulnerable of us all.

"There were two other girls in that van already. We saw them when they opened the door. She called me off." Z paced and put her hands in her hair.

I clamored back into the van. The rust from the decomposing

van metal flecked on my hands made the fact that they were shaking more obvious.

I ran back the video twice and missed the spot both times. Leto eased in behind me and Z hunched behind him. He cued up the part and had the peace of mind and clarity to pause it right when the kidnappers' van door was agape.

Two women. Not screaming, but definitely scared, were on the floor, huddled together.

"Shit." I watched the slow-mo of Aster's hand forming the sign that we had for roll with it.

If the plan changed and we needed the others to trust our split-second decision-making, that was the sign. Roll with it.

"Who had the communication?" Leto was already pulling up a FaceTime with T.

"I did. I still fucking do." Z slapped her forearm to indicate where the device was located. Her tasteful lily of the valley tattoo hid a secret. I had a similar procedure as well. In between our layers of skin, we each had a subdermal pocket surgically installed. We used it for our very small nonmetal communication devices. Aster couldn't get one—because she wasn't just allergic to shrimp. The ink in the device reacted with her skin when she had tried to get one installed.

"It should've been me." I hugged my center. The butterflies that had been warning me that something was going to go wrong turned into armed helicopters banging around on my insides.

"They didn't want me. Besides my fighting back. They only wanted her. I guess she was perfect for whatever they were looking for. And they already had two other girls." Z put a hand on my shoulder. She wasn't affectionate, usually. So this was her way of making me understand that she'd already cast me in Aster's role and rejected the idea.

"What do we do? We have to get her." I rolled the video back and started memorizing faces.

"She called me off, so we have to trust her. We go back, and we trust her." Z was talking a good game, but I noticed that her left eyelid kept twitching.

Maybe I'd been wrong. We'd completed our last mission by bringing in Max. Rescuing a houseful of girls was stupid. I was trying to extend our time together for selfish, non-practical reasons, and I was really hoping Aster wasn't going to pay for my mistakes with her life.

"Okay. Let's go home then. She's got her tracker on, at the very least. And her meds—

if they let her keep them."

Leto got in the driver seat and Z and I sat together in the passenger side—her sitting on my lap. The cargo space would have easily held her, but I wrapped my arms around her and rested my cheek on her spine. Z reached her hand around and put it on my head.

We were both terrified. It was like being a tiger in a cage, imprisoned and unable to attack.

I didn't like it. Not at all.

CHAPTER
TWENTY-FOUR

Aster

I t had been a quick decision. I saw their eyes and waved off
Z. There was no way I could leave these girls by themselves
in this van. It was a second. The split second before jumping
out of a plane. There's a safety mechanism in your brain that begs
you to stop.

It was like that, except my safety mechanism begged me to go.
I knew that I had the smallest window to be in that van with
them.

The Lady Mafia were too old for these men. Despite trying to
act vulnerable, it was something these types of predators could
smell. Sure, being on the shrimpies made me popped out and
twerky, but it also made me disorganized and hazy. That's why
these guys took me, I was betting.

All of Z and Indy's carefully laid plans were now shit. I knew
it when I saw how they held themselves around Z. These men
were cowards. They didn't take any chances at all, and a strong
woman like Z could only fake it for so long. I was out of my mind
on shrimp, but I still had a leg up on the terrified ladies in the van
with me.

I pinched my lips shut and did my best not to sing out or say
anything shrimp-like. I needed to concentrate, and fast. My inten-

tion was to save the ladies in the van, but as we rolled along, I realized that part of our plan was still good. I'd be able to expose where the island and the assholes involved were keeping their new victims, and maybe I would be able to identify other victims while under their control.

The douchebags were vaping like it was actually necessary to pump oxygen out of the cartridges. I slid my eyes to the smaller of the two victims. She was trying to free her wrists from the zip ties that were holding her hands behind her back. When she met my eyes, I gave her the smallest head shake and closed one eye to try to ward her off of her current activity.

The one next to her was ashen faced and in shock. *Don't whistle. Don't try to twerk. Don't think of cheating asshole ex-fiancé. No orgasms.* The driver took turns like a jerk. Every time we made a left, we hit our heads on the side of the van.

"You're going to damage the goods if you keep that up." He had a cool tone, but it carried confidence. Long beard and gauged ear holes.

He was either a hidden nice guy or the deadliest in the group. Time would tell—if we got time to play with.

"Yeah, yeah. As long as we can get between their legs, it'll be okay." The driver sneered in the rearview mirror.

I watched Beard Guy's eyes go shark-like and his jaw twitch. Faster than my shrimp brain could process, Beard was out of his seated position and squeezing the voice box of the driver with his left hand and taking over the steering wheel with his right.

"Fuckhead, what did I just say?" Beard wasn't wielding any weapons, but his voice held the dangers of a gun safe.

The driver made a noise that sounded like a kid stomping on a barely inflated balloon.

Beard was good at multitasking, keeping the van on the road and bringing the driver to the brink of death with ease.

After what felt like a good thirty seconds longer than I would have used to choke the guy out, Beard let go. The gasping breaths were accompanied by the driver's shoulders shaking.

Beard got close to his ear and hissed, "Drive like they're precious cargo or I'll rip your dick off and then use this very van to run it over."

The driver nodded over and over and wiped at the drool on his lips. "You got it, Cain." His voice had a rasp to it that could possibly be a permanent reminder of the correction he'd just received. He did change his driving, and my head appreciated it.

Of course, I could get out of these zip ties if I wanted. I was fairly certain I could get away, too, even shrimped up. But there was no way I could get both of these ladies free with me, especially with Cain the multitasker.

This was a good opportunity. Not ideal because with Z we would be able to wreck some face as soon as the island was revealed. But I wasn't a horrible alternative to nothing.

I settled back and rested. I would need energy for the shrimp comedown orgasms and for the taking on a ring of sex trafficking assholes.

TWENTY-FIVE

Z and Indy were oddly quiet. I mean, Aster was certainly the most talkative out of the three, but the familiar banter was missing and the silence felt hollow. Like the missing Aster's energy was a blackhole sucking all the content out of the air.

I was the driver while the ladies tapped on various electronic devices. What they had access to and what I had access to from my previous business was very different. Mercy must have supplied them because this high tech shit needed a lot of modifications. He was a legend at that, at least that was the rumor I'd heard. Certainly the compound we were staying at was tricked out.

"You get that last ping?" Indy broke the silence.

"Yeah. That's the longest bridge in the area. Miles long. Ten miles long. Where could they be headed?" Z clicked her tongue.

"I'll share this with T and see if she has any leads on the islands." Indy stopped typing long enough to give me a concerned glance. I didn't know why this bridge was a problem. And from the silence, I wasn't going to find out right away. I concentrated on driving.

When we finally got back to Mercy's compound, T and

Animal were already outside. She had a laptop open that she was typing on as she walked and Animal held out his arms to Zinny.

"It'll be okay. We're all in this. Aster comes back, I promise."

Tough as nails, Zinny melted into the big man's arms. T rubbed her back briefly before turning to Indy.

"We've got some leads in that area, and it's not great." She stepped closer to Indy to show her the screen.

"Oh. Great. So they have it fortified to Hell and back, I'm betting." Indy twisted her head one way and then the other. The layout on the screen must have had her perplexed.

I stepped behind them both and peered at the screen. "Oh shit." It was all coming together for me now.

The bridge led to another bridge in the middle of freaking nowhere. Beyond that, they would have to travel on a ferry boat or something. But I'd been there before on a dicey mission about a decade ago. They weren't trafficking people then, but drugs designed to look like makeup palettes. They must have changed courses, or added more specialties, as it were.

"I've been there," I added to the information we had.

Indy turned slowly and then looked me up and down. I held my chin up and flexed one hand out. I didn't want to disappoint her, and the sheer look of that emotion seemed to be her face's baseline.

Zinny stepped toward me. "What? Did you work for these people?"

She was itching for a fight. Her devastation over losing Aster to the kidnap van had her searching for an outlet. My balls were probably looking like great punching bags right about now.

These ladies were like knives. Highly effective, very sharp, and great weapons for killing people.

"In the beginning, that place was run by an older boss. He died of something..." I racked my brain for what it was. "It had to be like ten years ago. Shit."

Indy turned from me and back to the images on the screen.

It came back to me in a rush. "He died from falling off his

yacht. He was with his mistress and his other mistress. And he fell in and no one knew how to swim."

"That's a great story. Why were you there?" Zinny licked her lips.

"I was running the manufacturing plant that was there. I picked up the product and delivered it to either New York or Boston, depending on what it was." I held up both of my hands. "No people. I've never dealt in people."

Indy turned to face me with one eyebrow raised. She didn't have to say it. I knew I had to add, "Until you ladies. Of course."

Zinny shook her head and rolled her eyes. "Well, sit down and tell us what you know."

It took a combination of Google Earth photos and my memory to draw up a decent blueprint of what was going on.

Indy tapped the manufacturing plant. "This is my guess for where they keep a majority of the girls. Only a few windows, limited exits, and the ability to hold a large amount of people."

"I mean, yeah. It fits the bill. They also have a row of houses. We called them the minor buildings because they ringed the main house." I pointed at the screen.

Zinny twirled a knife in her hand. "They would use those as stopovers for the fuckheads that want to be with the kidnapped ladies—just a guess."

Indy squinted at the screen. "It would make sense. They could monitor who comes on the island, and then monitor the paying assholes. They might even be making blackmail tapes. They could do a lot of wrong on an island so private."

The knife that Zinny had been twirling was instantly lodged in the closed door. "I'm not letting them do that shit to Aster."

Indy reacted like having a weapon lodged in the only exit to the room was a valid opinion. "Agreed. But this place is locked down. We can't go in there balls first. We have to think this out."

"We can't sit on our hands waiting for Aster to die." Zinny pushed herself off the table.

"That wasn't what I said. We have a very obvious public

depiction of this place and the memory that Leto has intact after ten years. We have to imagine things have changed. Let's meet with Mercy and Animal and see if they know anything about it."

Indy sat in the desk chair.

"I hate that idea." Zinny was hot and ready to make a move.

"I know, but we trust Aster to handle herself. She wanted to take the chance, and I'm insisting it's for a good reason." She turned back to the computer and pulled up the text messaging. After a short back and forth, she had news. "They're on their way. They know about this island and have a few pointers."

Zinny cracked her knuckles before hissing in Indy's direction. She'd stopped fighting. This was the best way forward and she knew it.

ASTER

The shrimp orgasms had slowed the van's progress despite my best attempts to keep them quiet. Cain had watched me with his sharp eyes. Another man threatened to shoot me if I didn't stop all the panting. I couldn't stop even if I wanted to, and I hadn't wanted to. I realized the more off balance these men were, the better it was. They would make mistakes if they were distracted, and my throes of pleasure were doing a great job of that.

When the van careened into a spot in a Walmart parking lot, I knew I had successfully taken them off course. All Cain had mentioned was that he didn't want to be late and that they needed to get back to the island by dinner.

Now we somehow had time for a break where all the men evacuated the van like it was on fire, leaving me with the other two captives.

I let my head rest backward, knowing that my skin was flushed and glistening.

"Are you faking that?" one of the girls finally spoke up when the van was empty.

"No. I wish." My chest rose and fell with the effort.

"I've never seen anyone have that kind of alone me time as a side effect," the other girl spoke up.

"Well, now you have. How long have you been in this van?" We had a small window of time where the villains were out of earshot, and I needed to find out as much information as I could while I had the chance.

"It feels like forever," the first offered.

"I've had one overnight here, I think. It's so hard because the van is dark. And these blindfolds don't reveal much." The second shifted her weight from one hip to the other.

"I bet. We have to stick together because I want to get us all out of here." I heard the crunch of gravel and the door swung open.

Cain heaved himself inside and I watched through half-closed eyes.

"You done?" He seemed to have to sit down twice, like something was in the way. A gun. An excited dick. Maybe both.

"Probably not." Although I hadn't been faking, I certainly could let a pulsating faux climax roll through me if we needed it.

Cain held my gaze while the other men got into position. It wasn't a threat. It was something more. A tell. A peek at a poker hand. It took just a second, but he was warning me—of what, I wasn't sure.

He was going to be involved. This had happened to me before. It was like a déjà vu feeling. Like time travel. I knew that he would be in my way, a part of my decisions moving forward.

I knew that Cain and I were destined to have an intertwined fate where we were headed. I just wasn't sure if it was for good or evil. Looking for good in a kidnap van was probably stupid. I could hear Zinny in my head, telling me I needed to stop looking for a hero. And she would be right. I didn't have a mirror handy, but I was going to shrimp my way to saving these girls.

And Cain was either going to help or hurt. I was leaning toward help. I took a huge leap and gave him a purposeful wink. Then another orgasm built up again.

CHAPTER
TWENTY-SIX

Aster

When we finally pulled into the parking lot by the wharf, I knew we were going to have to change transportation. The van would not make it to the island. There was a small plane parked by a run-down looking runway.

I tried to gage whether Cain was scared or not. I felt my swelling starting to ease up. I needed another shrimp pill. Well, Indy would say I needed a Benadryl and an Epi pen, but this little delay trick of mine was my key to getting on the island.

I'd waved Zinny off. I knew she would be rolling mad wherever she was, but the truth was, I knew I had done the right thing.

Somehow, it made perfect sense for me to be heading to this place. The impending broken engagement with Spenser, kidnapping Max, all of it. Learning how to be an assassin. It was to bring me here to save these ladies.

I saw it clearly. I got Cain's attention and he leaned toward me.

"Hey, I have an allergy pill in my pocket. Can you put it in my mouth?" I tapped the small pocket in my jeans.

Cain looked from my face to my pocket and back again before deeming it a safe request. The Epi pens were rolled in the cuff of my jeans and secured with a few hand stitches. He had me lean back so he could stuff his thick finger into my pocket. He hooked a pill with his index finger and then took it out. He studied the pill for a few seconds before randomly sniffing it.

"Smells like fish." He held it out to me.

I put it on my tongue like I was receiving holy communion. I swallowed it down sans water, but it wasn't easy. My throat started to swell almost instantly.

Cain's eyebrows marched close together. "You okay?" His left eyebrow skyrocketed.

I concentrated on getting the pill down. My lips and butt started the process right away, and my throat did not like how long the shrimp pill had to stay in my throat. It was closing, too. Deep breaths through my nose were my only hope right now. I tried to slow my heartbeat, so the poison I was ingesting would not pump through me so fast.

My next few breaths came easier. I would live through this one. I nodded my thanks at Cain and he seemed to take it as the response he needed.

We were moving now anyway. A transfer from the van to the small plane. I was already hating the whole thing. Even more so when I saw the pilot was the spitting image of the van driver. I was hoping he didn't suck at flying as much as the van driver did at vanning.

Cain stayed near me while the other guys took the other women.

"You think he'll be mad that we only got three?" Van Driver was worried and loudly cluing us all into his concerns.

Cain scoffed. "Of course. He's always mad."

His hands went to my hips and he guided me to the back of the plane. There were too many people, so I had to sit on Cain's lap. The seatbelts were disregarded. I tried not to picture how many times I'd seen planes just like this crash. And always, it was a risk taking or faulty equipment that did them in.

We could barely hear each other when the plane engine

whirled to life. I leaned back against Cain's strong chest, feeling the warmth radiating from him.

"You going to do all that moaning and screaming again? Or do you think you can just sit pretty for this ride?"

His voice rumbled just behind my ear and sent pleasure waves through my hyper swollen body. "Shit."

The first of many strong orgasms was about to start. Cain was going to know me really well if we lived through this plane ride.

When we finally landed on the island, I had said every prayer I knew a few times over. I knew that Cain was packing more than weapons. He had a nice cannon in his pants and all my flailing around really let me know what he was dealing with. He was a good-looking man, but when he helped me up out of the plane seat, I took a longer look in his eyes.

He took a deep breath that flared his nostrils and made me whimper with an O aftershock. The shrimpies were an odd superpower.

When we all disembarked, I tried to get the lay of the land. It was a stunning location, of course. The water was crystal blue and the sand that rimmed the edges was a sparkling white. It was a combination that almost blinded me. There were little cottages dotting the beaches, each in a different color. It would give a resort vibe if it wasn't for the watchtowers and men walking around with AR-15s strapped to their backs.

Cain touched my elbow. A man in an all-white linen suit sauntered up the group of us. He had a toothpick in his mouth and twirled it from one side of his lips to the other.

"This is it?"

He was the boss. It was clear with how the men's body language changed. They were subservient now. Well, they all were except for Cain. He seemed to stand up taller.

"You can only fit so many on the plane, Cruz." A woman in a matching outfit catwalked onto the runway.

"We can always have a few of the guys catch the next plane, or they can swim. I have a host of new clients coming this weekend and they wanted more options." He waved his hand over us, using his wrist as if it was not actually attached.

We were to be menu choices. I felt my stomach roll. This was why I was here. Even if all I could do was put a stop to this, that would be something. This kind of evil perpetrated more evil. It was a haven for the bastards to do what they wanted and feel untouchable.

Cain's pinkie lightly touched mine, and I realized I had my hand in a tight fist. I let it relax. I didn't want to give myself up before I got to do some damage.

"Able, you always think you have all the answers, but I run the show. Don't make me tell Grandfather that you're acting up again." Cruz slid his sunglasses on top of his forehead and walked close to one of the van girls. He grabbed her jaw and twisted her head from one side to the other.

"She could be prettier. Couldn't you find someone prettier?" When he let go, I saw the fingermarks on her face.

It looked red enough that I thought there might even be a bruise soon.

"Hey. You're a fucking jackass." Oops. Shrimpies made my tongue do the things that got us both in trouble.

Cruz turned his head toward me. "Excuse me?"

Shit. I was all in now and lighting all my good plans on fire.

"I don't have an excuse for you. Why did you have to manhandle her like that?" I took a step toward him and Cruz countered with his eyes widening.

"You've got a mouth on you? I have ways of fixing that." He stepped toward me and pulled his arm back.

I braced myself for the smack. I would have to take it. I did some super quick captive calculations, and me fighting Cruz until he was wearing his balls as earmuffs would not help with my plans to get these girls off this island.

As Cruz's hand came toward my face, Cain stepped up and snatched Cruz's wrist with the speed of a rattlesnake.

"This one is mine," Cain hissed in Cruz's face.

I watched as Cruz did his own quick math. Cain was intimidating and seemed to have control of the guys around us. He had their respect at the very least.

Cruz scoffed and looked around. I watched as Able raised his eyebrows. That was enough to change Cruz's course of action.

"Fine. Whatever. She's too old anyway. And that's some horrible plastic surgery. You can have your broken doll, Cain." Cruz turned his back on us both. "Get these other two to intake. I want them ready by Friday night, and I need, like, at least another six. Maybe head down to Pottersville Road again. There has to be some new runaways."

As he walked away, Cruz kept talking about numbers and fresh meat. I hated him even more. No matter what happened, I had to make sure his time on this planet was short.

Cain put his hand on my upper arm and started walking us away. I stumbled a little and he caught me. He wrapped an arm around my waist.

"You still unsteady?" His voice was deep and close to my ear. I could feel his beard tickle the side of my neck.

"I usually am." I didn't clarify that I was unsteady during my allergic reaction, but on a normal day, I could keep my balance on a tightrope fifteen stories up.

We walked a short way to a light blue cabin on the beach.

"This is your place, but I'll stay with you."

It wasn't a request, it wasn't a suggestion, it was just the facts. He opened the door, and I noticed right away that there were no locks.

The cabin had an open floor plan. The only walls were around the bathroom, but the bedroom, the sitting area, and the small kitchen had a system of curtains set up from the rafters.

When Cain closed the door behind us, he motioned to the couch and I gratefully sat down. All that standing was taking a lot out of me. I was trying to process all this new, vital information while also monitoring my throat and heart rate.

And the amount of bounce my booty had. Another round of

shrimp pills would be a horrible idea, but I wasn't sure if a deflated Aster would make these guys want to make me walk the plank.

I imagined what was happening with the other new girls and ground my teeth together. This would be the tough part. Waiting. Letting things happen that I could conceivably stop so that we could get to the rescue.

Cain went to a blanket chest and popped it open. There were duffle bags and notebooks inside.

"So you knew we would be here?"

"I keep my stuff here." He pulled out a duffle bag.

"That doesn't answer my question, but let's go with it." I slumped over on the couch. I was running on fumes after all the orgasms.

He pulled out a pair of sweet pink sweatpants and a matching sweatshirt. "You can wear these if you want."

He set them down near my head. I reached out. They were as soft as a bunny's butt.

"Are they my size?"

"They'll fit." He was tapping away on his phone now. I rolled off the couch and bundled up the clothes. In the bathroom I switched out from the formfitting shirt I had on to the new clothes. I tucked my jeans and the lifesaving Epi pens on the small shelf by the shower.

The clothes were soft, and they did fit. Did he know I would be kidnapped? Were these for me, or was it just luck? When I came out of the bathroom, Cain was sitting on the couch waiting. He nodded when he saw me.

"Yeah. Fits." He rubbed his temple.

I sat down near him. I could feel my skin starting to tingle. I had a few hours left in me, and the baggy clothes would extend the amount of swelling I needed. It would be great to give my body a break from the hyper inflammation for a few hours.

It would help to know if Cain was a friend or an enemy. He was working for Cruz, so that immediately made me second guess him. But there was something about him that had a layer of trust-worthiness, which didn't make much sense. We were on an untraceable island where humans were trafficked. No one here was doing anything but going straight to hell.

Cain gave me a side-eye. "You hungry? I can take you over to the mess tent."

I shrugged. "I could eat."

He held out his hand and I took it. "Stay close to me. Trust no one."

I didn't ask him if he couldn't be trusted as well. I wasn't just going to assume that he was trustworthy, but I wanted him to be. I wanted my gut instinct to be correct about him.

"Mess tent? I thought that was a military term." I slid on the flip-flops at the door. They were big but worked.

"A lot of the guys here are ex-military or guys that wanted to be. Keeps them focused on the objective here."

I nodded. I wasn't going to ask any more questions because my mouth already had a mind of her own—calling Cruz a jackass, even if it was the truth.

"A dangerous group." I had to walk faster to keep up with Cain's long strides.

"Never forget it." When we got to the mess tent, it was a combination of a wedding tent and thrift store. The benches and tables had seen better decades, but the display cases and the cooking equipment were all top-notch. Cain picked us each a plate and handed me mine.

"It's like a buffet. Get whatever you want. They don't charge us or anything." He loaded his plate up behind me in line. I gravitated toward the breakfast foods.

I had pancakes, a glass of milk, and a pile of orange slices. Cain's plate strained under all the food he had loaded up on it.

We both sat at a light blue picnic table and set out our plates. While we inhaled our food, I kept accidentally kicking him under the small table.

Eventually, we both had mostly empty plates and glasses.

"I feel like I haven't eaten in two nights."

"When we have drama like this, it is very hard to keep a schedule," he offered while constantly surveilling the room we were in.

"What happens to the girls that I came in with?" I tried to find them in the mess tent, but I couldn't place any of them.

"They have to get tested. They have about a week before they are put in rotation." He ripped a piece of bread in half and used it to sop up some of the left over gravy on his plate.

Everything I had eaten rolled in my stomach. The word "rotation" instantly brought up my hate.

I watched one of the guys with a gun herd three ladies into the room. They should have been in college; instead, they were terrified.

"Eat," was the only comfort he offered them.

I felt myself imprinting on the girls. They reminded me of Zinny, Indy, and me. They were tangled together in a way that told me they did everything together. Even this.

The ladies made their way to the buffet. I stood and Cain copied me.

"I need dessert." I pointed to my stomach.

"You just ate enough food to stock a small store. You can't fit anymore in." He tilted his head toward me.

"I can fit a lot of things." I gave him a saucy wink.

He huffed but followed me to the food. I walked next to the closest girl. She was hugging her plate to her chest like a stuffed animal.

"Hey." I tried to put warmth in the greeting. She turned to me with distrustful eyes. Oh, I recognized that look. I had that for a lot of years.

She took her plate away from her chest.

I held out my hand and smiled. "What are you interested in? I just ate a huge plateful and the food is safe."

The other two girls peered around each other taking me in. I gave them a little wave.

The girl next to me cleared her throat. "I love pancakes."

"Great. This food is all free. Let's make these fuckers pay out the ying-yang." I took her plate and piled four thick pancakes onto it.

Cain stood behind me, rocking on his heels with his thumbs in his pockets. "You know, meat is the most expensive thing to get and keep on the island."

I looked over my shoulder at him. Again, those good vibes. "Thanks Cain."

I turned back to the pancake lover. "You eat meat?"

She shook her head. "Today I do."

I gave her sausage and bacon and added a bit of ham at the end. I handed her plate back to her.

The asshole who had herded them into the mess tent came close. "Hurry the fuck up. I haven't eaten yet."

Cain leaned toward him. "Eat up, man. I got these girls for now."

I watched as the asshole narrowed his eyes, but then listened, grabbing his plate and pushing past the girls.

After taking two plates each, and grabbing cold waters, Cain led us to a bigger table. I sat down with the girls and Cain stood over us like he was keeping us there. I had a sense he was just making sure we had our space.

I pulled my hair back and twisted it into a bun. "I'm Aster and I was brought here yesterday."

The pancake lover introduced herself. "I'm Millie. That's Sandra and she's Dara. We got here last week. This is supposed to be our first night. That's what they said anyway."

The three girls swallowed and made eye contact with each other.

Cain leaned forward. "It would be a shame if you went to the bathroom and came down with the flu tonight, and Aster witnessed it." Then he rocked back on his heels.

I pouted my lips.

"That would be a shame. And then if you needed me to look after you, I mean, I wouldn't want any of the guys with

146

guns to get sick." I twirled my index finger, pointing around the room.

Millie lifted her eyebrows hopefully.

Sandra reminded me of Zinny with how quickly she plotted out the mission. "Bet they have cameras in the bathrooms."

"They do. But they did go down last week and the parts are coming from overseas, so it'll be a while." Cain said his piece and then walked away. It would be too suspicious if he was having a conversation with us like we were at a cocktail party.

I turned to Sandra. "I think he's trustworthy, but go with your gut. It's the thing that you can trust the most."

Dara leaned forward, almost getting her long brown waves in the syrup. Sandra fixed Dara's hair without even thinking about it. Oh my heart. They reminded me so much of my girls.

"Why are you helping us?" Dara squinted at me like she was trying to see through me.

I shook my head. "I'm not with them."

I didn't want to say too much. The bathroom didn't have a working camera, but the mess tent probably did.

The whole thing was dangerous, but this was a good group to get in touch with. I needed to try to get as many girls notified that I was trying to help as I could. Until Zinny and Indy could make a decent plan.

Not having the communication with my girls was hard.

After Dara accepted my short answer, she and the other girls seemed to think Cain's plan of getting "sick" was a way to put off their first night in the rotation.

I got up when they got up, after finishing their meals. Asshole popped by when we moved, but Cain was on it, telling him about our bathroom intentions.

In the mess tent, there was a public style bathroom with three stalls. Each girl took one and then did their best puke and fart impressions. I had to pinch my cheeks with my teeth to avoid bursting out laughing. Despite how stressful this situation was, they were really trying to make each other laugh. It was healing.

Another woman walked into the bathroom. I watched her face pale as she heard all the noises the girls were implementing.

"They aren't feeling well." I held open my palms toward the stalls. Then I had a thought. "They might not even be able to be in rotation all week. I hope you don't have it. It would be hell if this whipped through the island like the norovirus on cruise ships." I folded my arms in front of my chest and watched as the suggestion I planted reach her with its possibilities.

"You know, I've been feeling nauseous." She ran her hand over her stomach.

"You should ask anyone you know how they are feeling. I mean, shutting down rotation would be expensive and inconvenient." One of the girls managed to make a puke fart noise at the same time.

"You know? I better ask them." She rushed out of the bathroom. By the time all three girls were done, their bathroom exploits were clear to the whole mess tent.

The men with guns had their shirts covering their nose and mouths. I helped the girls out the front door and Cain was close behind. Asshole was nowhere to be seen.

The three girls showed me where their cottage was. It was three down from mine. Well, mine and Cain's. When they were settled, Cruz was banging on the door. Cain was waiting outside and had lazy eyes, but I could tell he was on edge.

The girls grabbed their stomachs or their heads and I stood to greet him.

"Hey, I'll never forget the first time we met, but I'll keep trying." I gave him a sickly sweet smile.

"Why are your tits so small?" Shit. The shrimpies. They were wearing off.

"Because I'm in a sweatshirt. Do you even know about clothes?" I put my hands on my hips and stuck my chest out to make it look bigger.

"You get here, and now all the women on the island are shitting their pants? How is that possible?" He took one step into the cabin, but then stepped back out when one of the girls made a fart sound.

"I'm a wizard, Harry. Clearly." I rolled my eyes. Cruz was a dumbass, but he was picking up on the fact that I had ulterior motives, even if he couldn't figure them out yet.

"How many girls we got for tomorrow?" Cruz turned to Cain, his neck veins pulsing.

"I have no idea. I've been monitoring these ones." He jammed his thumb in my direction.

"You know, sometimes cruise ships have to just park in the center of the ocean and just let the people be sick over the sides for like a week. If I were you, I'd be on the safe side and close it down." I leaned against the doorframe.

Cruz growled in the back of his throat. "We have you and the other new girls. And the preggos can work. Some of them anyway."

"Billionaires love when a person pukes on their dick. It's great for business." I was taking a stab in the dark—who I thought their clients were for these trafficked girls. Never mind that they also had pregnant girls on the island, for what purpose I wasn't sure, but it still gave me the shivers.

Cruz took another step backward. "The second I laid eyes on you, I knew you would be trouble. Lots of fucking trouble."

I lifted my eyebrows and my shoulders. "I certainly hope so."

Cruz titled his head to the left and gave me a small headshake.

Cruz stomped away from the cabin, digging his cell phone out of his pocket. "Get me the doctor on the goddamn line. Well, wake him up."

When Cruz was far enough away, I turned back to the girls. "I hope you guys feel better soon and this doesn't turn into a long-drawn-out illness. The good news is, there are cameras, so if you need help, I'm sure they can send someone."

It was just my way of telling them to keep up the farce. Staying sick meant staying safe. For now. The more time I bought Zinny and Indy, the better.

Cain and I headed back to our cabin once the girls were tucked in for the night and comfortable. We heard some retching as we walked back to our cabin.

He was doing things to help us. I just had to hope it was for good reasons. Cain and I were going to have to have a conversation.

CHAPTER
TWENTY-SEVEN

I should feel better about the plan. We had the best in the business crowded around a table. There was the last bit of intel Max was ever going to give us because it took a lot to get it out of him. But apparently, his brother worked on the island. He was in charge of maintenance, which sounded mundane and far too resort-based for a crime island.

But it had to happen. There were sheets and clothes and things needed to run smoothly when there were visitors there. I hated that they were called visitors. I hated that I had to time things a certain way.

Max's brother Berkley had a girlfriend he adored. Her long brown hair and height were just about equal to mine. Nieve and Berkley lived on the island, but every Sunday she made her way back onto the mainland to go to church with her family. Berkley would sometimes come with, and he insisted she cover up to go in and out so no man would ogle her.

He was possessive and dumb, but that would work in my favor. Zinny wanted to come as well, but I needed her on the outside. Her protection of Aster and me would be a superpower. She would be laser-focused on saving us. I knew Aster would want to save everyone she could. I wanted to save Aster and had a healthy dose of empathy for the victims. And Zinny would blow up the entire world to keep Aster and I alive.

Even with the backup of Mercy and his crew, I had concerns. The way this place was fortified and protected, we almost needed an airstrike. The local government was bought and sold. Everyone benefited from the island—except the victims.

I tried to swallow the burning. This was all too much. We weren't heroes. We weren't the ones you called when you needed help. We were tactical weapons.

It was like Zinny could hear my thoughts and we locked gazes. We had a conversation. The whole thing. My concerns. The ways the plan could go sideways.

Zinny shrugged. "She waved us off."

Slowly nodding, I committed to the mission. The outcome. All of it. If Aster thought this was worth doing, then it was all for one, one for all. I felt my mind close around the plan and lock it down like an Iron Man-style mech suit.

Doubt led to mistakes. I had to power through. Confidence was key. Zinny was already there—at that point.

We had three days to somehow use this information about Berkley to get on the crime island that seemed like it was the gateway to Hell.

When Zinny and I locked eyes, I knew she was thinking the same thing I was. That Aster hadn't been alone since we were all in the foster homes together. I mean, there were times she was with boyfriends or horrible Spenser, but for the most part, we were close so we could monitor her allergies. Her freaking potentially life-threatening allergies.

We would put our heads down and plan. Practice. Train. Both Zinny and I handled stress the same way. Acquire things. Knowledge, skills, weapons. The more stressed we were, the more rounds we went at each other during exercise.

Leto was a quiet rock. Providing water, holding punching bags, getting sandwiches. Going down on me to take the trapped look out of my eyes. Zinny was busy with a few of Mercy's men.

No single one could take her mind off her mission. But a few could, for a little while.

In our planning meeting with Nix, Animal, and T, they let us know that they were assembling a swarm of armed helicopters to be at our disposal. They couldn't help as much, because they had their own issue, but they could supply us with guns and ammo. And we would take it.

Zinny sat back in her chair when we ended the call, hands in her hair. "So best-case scenario? We get to Aster and toss her in a helicopter. Get us the hell out of there."

"We don't know how many girls there are. Hopefully, Nieve, the girlfriend, would be able to add to what we know, but Aster's not going to think this was worth it unless we save people." I pulled my feet under my chair.

Zinny ran her hands down her face. "How many people can fit in a helio?"

"A few. But we may have to plan on holding down the fort until we can get a large number of people off the island." I tried to imagine what we were dealing with. How well fortified they were.

This crime island was a playground for the worst humans in the world. It would be protected in ways we couldn't even imagine.

Hell, it wasn't even on any map we could find. Not even a whisper about it on the dark web.

Leto wrapped his knuckles on the door as he opened it. "Ladies, we have some images to show you."

He held out an iPad. Information on Max's brother Berkley's girlfriend was what we needed now.

Someone had pulled up the security camera from the liquor store across from the church.

Zinny took one look and tossed up her hands. "Fuck."

Out of the two of us, I could pass as the girlfriend. I had the same hair color, a similar body, and most importantly, a similar height.

"It's gotta be me, Z." I handed the iPad back to Leto.

"I know, and I hate it." Zinny stood and strode past Leto. She wanted to be the one to go in guns blazing. She would have loved to have me hang back. Then she could go rogue and extract Aster and to hell with the rest of the world.

It was setting fire to the edges of her hopes, but it made sense. In some way I knew that fate was right. I had to be the one that went undercover on the island.

Leto put out his hand and helped me out of the chair. He wrapped his arms around me and kissed the top of my head. "I would rather it was her going as well."

I gave a halfhearted chuckle against the nape of his neck. "Surrounded by these morally gray characters is exhausting."

"We like to keep you on your toes. And naked, if we had our dithers." He leaned down and brushed his lips across mine.

"No one says dithers. Sweet crap, that word just gave me the full body shivers." I emphasized it with a little shake.

"I'm naming our first dog Dithers," he said it louder this time.

I shook again. "You're going to really regret that when he runs away and you have to yell that over and over in the neighborhood to get him back." I rested my palms on his shoulders.

"Are our kids upset?" A future flashed over his handsome face.

He was risking things by picturing more than we had ever discussed. I played along. Because I could kind of see the white picket fence as well. Just a shimmering ghost of one anyway.

"All three. They're so upset. Dithers is such a nimrod." I smiled at his upturned lips.

"Oh yeah? What do we got? Three girls? I'd be the best girl dad ever." He pulled me closer until my feet were off the floor.

I kicked out a leg. "Oh, right? We have two girls and a boy in between. That last one had the biggest head so we had to stop after her."

"Are you sure my giant dick hasn't been training you up like a football team for the Super Bowl?" He rolled his hips against me and my feet flopped around.

"Maybe so. I forgot about all that good good." I smiled at him.

"Don't get my hopes up, even if we're joking." Leto frowned a bit.

"Hey, let's wait for hopes until after I get Aster back. Then we can hope all you want." I ran my knuckles over his jaw.

"Yeah. For sure. That's the kind of odds I'm used to. Let's infiltrate the most secretive, vile island on the face of the earth and liberate any and all prisoners, and then we can plan a future." He ran his hands down my arms.

"Simple as that, handsome." I took a step away from him. "Now come to the training session and do your best to stab and attack me so I stay sharp."

"Anything for you, gorgeous."

I saw the concern in the tick of his jaw. I pushed past it, then him to head to the space we had to get ready for Berkley's religious girlfriend to go to church.

LETO and I were wrapped in the sheets. Somehow they had wound themselves through our limbs like a puzzle.

"I guess we have to stay here now." He wasn't in any rush to get us out of bed.

I mostly handled my stress and worry with overplanning, over training, and over sexing. Leto was down for all of it.

I couldn't get to my phone, but it was vibrating off the end table with notifications.

"That's going to be Z with updates on the transportation and weapons for release day."

So far, if everything went according to plan, I'd be on the island for about a day. My job would be to inform T and Z about the optics. I'd use my tattoo hidden communication to pass the exact location and the number of unfriendlies on the island. My job was to save Aster and as many victims as I could. Then we would be swinging in with a highly trained group of Mercy guys. And Z would be armed and angry.

Until then, all I could do was research Nieve and her family. I had doubts she was willingly in a relationship with Berkley. Everything Max touched was evil as fuck. I wasn't looking to hurt her, but she would need to give us all the info she could. And she would have to stay with us until the island was dust.

When Sunday finally came around, I was anxious and keyed up. It was a full-time job not picturing what was happening to Aster. Zinny got me aside as I packed my bag to go to the church.

"Hey." She ran a finger over my tattoo that hid my communication device.

"Yeah." I tapped on the place on my skin as soon as her finger vacated.

"I can hear you. It's good." Zinny looked me over tactically. She wanted to make sure all the things I was doing made sense. We'd learned that getting back to the island was a one plane show, and I had to be a different person for God knew how long. It couldn't be really more than an hour because the amount of fuel the Cessna could carry, but it could always refuel somewhere. Unlikely, but still. We had run all the contingencies over and over, even the stupid ones.

Zinny chewed her bottom lip in an uncharacteristic hesitancy.

"Just tell me, Z." I needed to hear whatever was eating her up.

"This is the hardest job we've ever done. You've been persevering. I've been persevering. You have to get this right. I trust you. You're amazing. It's just you *have* to get it right." Her eyes almost rimmed in tears.

I grabbed her up and pulled her in for a hard hug. "I got it. I got you. It's okay.

We slapped each other's backs and then rubbed them. When we broke, we couldn't say any more to each other. We would possibly cry, and emotions had no place in today. We were weapons and needed to treat ourselves as such.

When Leto was ready, I had to put it in motion. My muscles ached from all the training. My mind was swimming with the things that needed to happen, but Leto took my hand and we started our walk to the church. In my big purse I had the makings of Nieve's possible outfit. I would take parts of her current outfit off of her if I had to. But first, we had to get there.

"What's going on up there?" Leto pointed to my head.

"Just calculations, predictions, and doomsday scenarios, so the usual." I rubbed my thumb over his knuckles, grateful to have him. It made me smile despite everything.

"Why am I so lucky to see those shiny white teeth?" He leaned down and kissed me mid-step.

"I think this happened between you and me despite ourselves." I squeezed his hand.

"Well, you just went ahead and made my damn day. You going to be my girl after all of this is over?" Now I got to see his full smile, eyes twinkling.

"It's a real possibility. I'm getting kind of addicted to this, to you." I rubbed his bicep with the hand he wasn't holding.

He pulled me to a stop, face serious. "Hey, live through this, okay? That's all I ask."

I touched his cheek. "Every intention of doing just that."

It felt like dust on my tongue. It felt like a lie. I pushed past it and smiled at him.

I was grateful Zinny couldn't see me or she would have noticed the change in a hot minute. Something was going to go wrong. I could feel it. Normally, I'd pull out. Cancel anything, everything if I got this feeling. But that was not an option today. Aster was depending on me.

LETO

I was so crazy about Indy I couldn't take it. She was so much more than any woman I'd ever met. She was a general, a badass, a sexy beast, and mine. I mean, I think she was mine. I had to get her to the plane. Well, stalk her from a distance once she had assumed Nieve's identity. Zinny would pick Nieve up at the church after the swap was made.

Indy and I took the church steps and then I held the door for her. We both acted like devoted parish members. We took a pew and pulled down the kneeler. There were a few other early birds. We would have to sit through Mass, and then there would be weekly confession.

We had scoped out the church a few times, so we knew that the confessionals were the old-fashioned full door kind. Inside, there was a wood partition that could be pulled aside. That was where we would do our worst work.

Indy was the perfect picture of a church going lady as Mass started. She knew when to stand, sing, and kneel. I followed her cues so I wouldn't look out of place. Finally, when Mass was over, most parishioners left. It wasn't a particularly crowded Mass, and only a few stayed behind for confession. One of these people was Nieve. We had studied the photos of her until I had to remind myself that she had never seen me. We weren't friends and I didn't know her.

Indy touched my arm before heading to the bathroom. I knew she would not really get there, but swing back.

Indy would loosen the vent in the hall behind the confessional. My job was to get into the booth just before Nieve.

I waited for the short line to form, then I stood next to her. She had a scarf wrapped around her head and was wearing sunglasses inside.

"Hey, can I slip in here? I have to get to work and I don't want to miss out." Nieve didn't say anything, but she nodded and motioned to the space in front of her.

I waited my turn and practiced keeping my breath even. I started thinking about my brother randomly. Matt was still a captive, but he had been helping do some coding for the organization he was with. So while I was with the Lady Mafia, he was at least protected.

Then it was my turn. When I closed the confessional door, I felt guilty as the kindly priest offered up, "Child, tell me your sins."

"Well, Father, there's this one I'm about to do—a real doozy." I slid the confessional door open and then reached into my pocket. I had a needle in his neck before he could gasp. The plunger was down and the chemicals were taking effect.

Watching the man slip boneless into the seat was sad. I took comfort that he would wake up in about forty-five minutes with a headache. Chances were, in the hospital. Because as soon as Indy had a handle on the situation, we would sound the alarm.

I waited as Indy shimmied through the vent. She didn't give me a kiss because she already had on Nieve's ever-present red lipstick. Her outfit was perfect, but no scarf.

I pointed to her head. Indy shook hers and whispered, "I'm going to take hers, and her sunglasses."

I passed her the remaining syringe.

"Good luck." I kissed the top of her head and went out of the confessional. Indy stood in the shadows in the small space as I held open the door for Nieve.

I had a pretend coughing fit as soon as I closed the door behind her so that the small ruckus of Indy injecting Nieve wouldn't be heard in the cavernous space of the church.

When Indy stepped out, seconds later, I saw that Nieve was covered with a black blanket, making her almost invisible. Indy closed the door and ran to the priests.

"Help him! The priest!"

She flung open the door and the three people remaining in line gasped. I waved my hands in mock panic. "Call 911. Shit, call 911."

"I'll go wait outside for the ambulance." Indy was wrapped in Nieve's scarf and had on her glasses. I followed her at a short clip and watched as she got into a black SUV with tinted windows. Just as the SUV pulled away, I heard the sirens in the distance.

Zinny appeared in a sedan and I hopped in.

"How'd it go?" She looked in the rearview mirror.

"Like clockwork. She's on her way." My stomach clenched hard. Now was the part where I let go. Zinny and I watched from a distance, listening to the music that was playing in Indy's SUV. At least we could still hear her.

As of right now, it didn't sound like there were any issues. Indy had passed the first challenge as Nieve. Next, she would have to pass on the plane as well.

We trailed behind, knowing where they were headed. After we parked where we could watch them, but they couldn't see our car, I listened as the possible love of my life climbed into a pretty crappy looking plane. No one made Indy. She just seamlessly infiltrated the plane. She was in the air in no time, and that was that. My girl was gone. The only information we would have now would be what she told us herself.

TWENTY-EIGHT

Aster

The amount of times that all of the girls pretended to get sick was almost incalculable. Cruz was losing his mind. And I knew that hopefully we would hear something from Zinny and Indy soon. Because this was a powder keg ready to explode. Especially if we were all discovered to be faking it. Cain had convinced Cruz that the virus didn't have a fever, so the symptoms were gastrointestinal and exhaustion. It was buying us time, and that's all I wanted.

Sunday afternoon, Cain and I were watching a movie. He promised me there were no functioning cameras or listening devices in my cabin. I believed him. The night before we were two bottles of wine into the evening when he told me why he was really here.

I'd poured us another round and set the bottle on the coffee table. We were both sitting on the floor with our backs against the sofa.

He started first. "You know, I really thought it would be here that I'd find her."

I turned to look at him, from his eyes to his lips to his eyes again.

"Yeah, I know I don't talk much. But it's just a night like this?

It was her favorite growing up. She loved Saturdays. Birthday Party days were what she called them when we were growing up. Even if no one had a birthday, she'd have her party dress on and wrap her own presents. Man, I loved that kid."

If I knew anything about men, it was to let them talk if they were on a memory train.

"I just had her to watch as a kid. She was my responsibility. Sure, I was older, but she was just the sun and the damn moon. I left for the military, and she took it hard. But when I got word that she had disappeared, I almost didn't believe it."

"You've been looking for your little sister?" I took a sip of my wine.

He set his wine glass down and threaded his hands behind his neck. "I've been to the worst places in the world. I've found places and people that no one even knows exist. Just to find her. I'm amazing at finding people. It's what I specialize in. I can find anyone, but I can't find her."

He looked at the ceiling.

"How old was she when she went missing?" I set my glass down, too.

"Seventeen. Tough age because the police really think she's a runaway. I knew it was different. She loved our house. Our place. My mom said that Clara had gotten in trouble a few times because I was gone. She missed me and wanted attention. Sometimes I have panic attacks thinking about where she is and I can't move. I can barely breathe."

I touched his knee. "Hey, I'm sorry. If I can help after we get out of here, I will."

He gave me a funny look. "Thanks. I mean, I appreciate it, but like, what can you do?" He wiped his eye with the back of his hand.

"I know a few people." I wasn't ready to give up our whole organization just yet, but I would try to help him find Clara. It was the least I could do.

I knew he was putting his neck on the line for the other girls and me. He was tipping me off on camera and recordings and backing up our faux sickness.

I leaned over and cupped his cheek. "How did you wind up here, of all places, being a good guy?"

The tenderness in him spoke to me. I brushed my finger on his beard. It was soft. I leaned over and gave his jaw a sniff.

"You always smell good."

He was stiff all of a sudden. Like a statue. Like I was a poisonous snake.

I backed off. "You okay? I'm sorry. I'm sort of a toucher."

He slowly turned toward me, desire in his gaze. Maybe there was nothing sexier than a scary looking man's face when he was hot on a lady. And that lady was me. No shrimpies. Deflated down to my normal size. He took his hand and circled it in a ball.

He took a deep breath through his nose and exhaled through a whistle.

We sat in silence for a few seconds, then he broke it. "Miss Aster?" He looked away from my face like he was going to say something he was ashamed of. "You're the ..."

He stopped and readjusted. This intimidating, commanding man was nervous. It was adorable. I bit my lip.

"Prettiest I've ever seen. Please don't touch me. My body needs to try with you and I won't let it. This place is so evil." He swallowed hard.

"Hey. Let me tell you something about me. I believe life is the moment you're in. Everything else is wet cotton candy. Gone." I scooted closer again, now that I knew what was wrong. "Do you have a crush on me?"

Cain side-eyed me and then tipped his head once.

"Can I touch you?"

He was a wall of a man. A mountain of a person.

"If you want to. I would...enjoy that." His other hand curled into a ball.

"I'm just here in sweats and stuff. You cool with that?" I

leaned closer for another sniff. He was divine smelling, but you had to be close to get the subtle scent.

He turned to me, his lips grazing my forehead. "You're literally the most favorite thing my eyes have ever seen. I mean, you're not a thing. You know. Lady."

"This nervous version of you? I want to ride it." I straddled him and he moved his hands out to the sides, still balled up.

He looked to his lap and then up to the ceiling. "You don't have to do this. I'm going to help and protect you no matter what."

I tilted my head to the side before tipping his chin down. "I know. You have to understand that I wouldn't ever do anything like this unless I wanted to."

Cain cleared his throat.

I added, "This is a deadly situation. I'd love to have a few really lovely orgasms, just in case things go sideways."

Cain's eyes went wide. "I can make that happen. Or die trying."

He ripped my sweatpants and panties off like he was angry at them. "Okay?"

Permission requested. "Yes, please."

I loved that he was frantic. Dying to taste me. Me. Just like this, like how I was. No false stuff. No puffiness that would fade.

He laid me down like I was made of glass, but ate me out like he had something to prove to my ancestors. He kneeled between my legs and face-planted.

I'd never come so quickly before. His fingers and tongue found ways inside of me that had his name on them. Whenever I tried to get to him, to offer some sort of reciprocation, he would do something else. Touch somewhere else. He was not stopping until I was a flopping sop of a human.

When he had finally deemed me finished, he sat back and wiped his mouth with the back of his hand. "I've never tasted someone that was exactly the right spice for me. Until you."

"Let me get to you. You still have your damn pants on." I
sat up.

Gone was Mr. Nervous. He stood and undid his belt buckle.
The zipper on his dark jeans was straining. I had my gaze locked
on his crotch, so he took his shirt off next.

"Tease," I murmured.

When he took off his shirt, he was covered in tattoos. He was
not ripped, but he was crazy strong. Like the same build as the
guys that sometimes lifted boulders in kilts.

He had to weigh so freaking much. He was a brickhouse.

Next, he undid his zipper and let the jeans slide to his knees. I
grabbed the center and pulled him to me. He was hairy, but neat.

"Well, Coke can, what's up?"

He was a reasonable length but the girth made all kinds of
promises. He gave me a low chuckle that turned into a groan as I
licked and sucked on him. He was adorable and sexy and my kind
of guy.

I let him feel all my tricks. The humming, the gargle suck, and
even the nibble. When he came, he had his hands on his hips and
a shout in his throat.

I swallowed quickly. He fell to his knees. "Miss Aster? So
pretty."

He was back to being nervous and I felt proud of myself. He
was a good one. Somehow, I felt like he was a gift from the
universe just for me.

He stood and pulled me from my spot on the couch.

"We're going to rehydrate, and then I'm going to put it to you
until you're done with orgasms."

It took all night. Until there was a knock on my cabin door.
Cain was up with his gun ready at the same time as I stood.

He peeled the curtain back to peek. "Huh. That's Berkley's
girlfriend."

As he unlocked the door, I knew. I knew it had to be one of
my girls.

When the door was fully opened, Indy, dressed in a scarf and jeans, was in front of me. I reached out for her hand and pulled her inside.

We were wrapped in each other's arms as Cain closed the door behind her.

"You know Nieve?" He was thoroughly perplexed.

I pulled down Indy's scarf.

"You're alive. And you're not puffy. I buried you so many times in my head." Indy pushed my hair away from my face. "I've got her. She's here."

Indy was using the communication device she had hidden behind her tattoo, but Cain didn't know that.

"What a minute, who are you talking to?" He stepped closer.

"He safe?" Indy seemed skeptical.

"He is." I turned to Cain. "She's safe, too. This isn't Nieve. This is Indy, my sister."

Cain holstered his gun and scratched his head. "Uh. yeah. Still not piecing this together yet."

Indy ignored him. "What do we know so far?"

I pulled her to the couch and unloaded all the information I had gathered so far. It took a long enough time before Cain finally sat down in the chair opposite from the couch.

The number of victims, the locations, and how the outbuildings were set up. I knew that anything I said to Indy would be broadcast to Zinny and beyond.

Finally, Indy nodded. "You did great, kiddo. Proud of you. You and that amazing photographic memory."

Cain leaned forward. "That's great. I'm proud of both of you. Can someone please tell me what the ever-living shit is going on here?"

Indy stood up and put her finger to her lips. I rose from the couch, instantly alert. Cain was smart enough to keep quiet. We eventually all heard what had caused Indy's reaction.

"She was supposed to head back to Berkley's place. But she just...took off. I don't know, Berkley's kind of a pussy, but I still don't want him to show up at home tomorrow without his damn girlfriend waiting."

The words and the men speaking them faded out.

Cain turned to Indy. "So you took Nieve's place on the plane? When she went to church?"

"Did you shoot up a church?" I was scared that Indy was going to damage the inroads I had been working on with God. I'd been praying since we were kids.

Indy shook her head. "No. God, no. I just drugged the priest and the girlfriend. It was fine. They're fine."

"How's Z taking me being here?" I was actually surprised that it was Indy and not Z here in the flesh.

"She's feral about it. You know her. She's going to burn the whole world down until we are back together." Indy pointed at her wrist tattoo, reminding me that we had ears in other places. Most importantly, the very lady we were discussing. "There was only one shot to get someone here and I fit the bill." Indy turned back to the door, looking at it. "How long do you think we have before they turn the place upside down for Nieve?"

Cain held up his index finger and stood. "Right now no one is saying anything on the comms, so I think the transportation guys are trying to keep the whole thing down low. Losing Berkley's girlfriend is a problem, and it could have severe consequences."

"Yeah, these human traffickers can shove all the fucks I give right up their assholes." Indy started looking around the cabin.

"Well, you probably have until morning, and I'll keep you posted on what they're saying." Cain tapped his earpiece.

"That's awfully nice of you." Indy walked up to him and stood toe to toe. "You care to tell me why you are being so cool to us?"

Cain looked down his nose at Indy. She was shorter than him, but she had the demeanor of a lady that always got her way. The matriarch of an Italian family combined with the head nurse at an ER.

"Because Aster is special and I want to save someone. I can't find my sister, and if I don't do something meaningful, I'm going to lose my mind." He folded his arms in front of his chest.

Indy narrowed her eyes. "Hey. Sorry to hear that. I trust you because she trusts you. I can also kill you before you even know it's going to happen, so stay on the right side of wrong for me, okay?" She reached out and fixed the collar of his shirt.

His smile lifted on one side. "You got it."

Indy turned back to me. "We've got a long night ahead. If Berkley gets back and sounds the alarm, we'll lose the element of surprise. Zinny is going to have to move Heaven and Hell and get the troops in here tomorrow."

"Tomorrow? That's really quick. I need to get info out to a lot of ladies." I tried to do the math of it all. At least twenty girls that came to the mess hall, five ladies that were pregnant. Plus, the three girls I helped pretend they were sick.

Cain sat down and tapped his fingers on the coffee table. "I may know of a place where we could stash them all. Because there's no way we can move them off the island without being seen, but we could hide them on the island."

Indy pulled on my arm and we both sat down. "Let's hash this out. I want us to be ready for anything tomorrow."

I put my arm around her. "Man, am I glad to see you."

Indy leaned close. "I've got a few more of those travel Epi pens and a comm for you, but I'm going to need a bathroom and a few glasses of wine to get them for you."

"Not the dick holster?" We had things we did when we had to in life.

Indy tilted her head and winked. I had hope now. Indy was here, and Z was orbiting somewhere, in touch and prepared.

This place was vile, and putting an end to it seemed like the most important thing in the world to do.

LETO

The place that we took Nieve to was arranged by Zinny. Two other guys and I were cautious with her but careful. There was a chance that Nieve was a victim, and we weren't about to re-traumatize her.

Z apparently had the same thought, because she walked through the door, pulling off her driving gloves.

She started in immediately. "How long has she been out?"

I gave her a quick answer. "This is about two hours in a few minutes."

Z went to the first aid kit. We pulled out an alcohol swab and cracked it open. She waved it underneath Nieve's nose a few times until finally the woman's eyes started blinking. As she focused on the room, she startled.

Z put her hand on our captive's shoulder. "You're safe. These guys listen to me, and all we need from you is information."

Nieve's eyes grew wide, and then she covered her mouth.

"I don't feel well." Her mumbled words came from around her fingers.

Z opened a fresh alcohol wipe.

"Sniff this, it'll help. Understand that it will pass in just a few minutes. We were very careful with the dose that we gave you that rendered you unconscious so that we could bring you here to talk to you safely."

It was interesting to see Z in a soothing mode, one female to another. She usually had a rough edge to her. I couldn't tell if she was faking it or if she was genuine. I was mostly guessing it was real, but I bet it depended on Nieve's answers to her questions.

Z returned to me. "You're monitoring the comms right now. Indy is there and Aster is okay. We're gonna have to move quickly. The information we get from Nieve can help us, but I'm gonna need you to verify as much of it as possible."

I nodded and pulled up to the laptop that was near the first aid kit. The abandoned store that was set up for us to do this inquisition in was drafty and dusty, but it had what we needed, thanks to Z thinking ahead.

Nieve took a few deep breaths with the small cloth in front of her nostrils until she started to nod. "That's better. I feel better."

Z took to one knee. "I'm glad to hear it and I'm sorry that we had to get you out of there the way we did, but we wanted to make sure that you had a way to return to your life if you had to."

I thought it was odd and popped an eyebrow in Z's direction. She rolled her eyes at me. "You never know how many fireballs a woman has to juggle and how many people depend on her especially in a situation like this. I want to make sure she has all the options she needs."

Then Z turned back to Nieve. "I hope you realize that I've put your needs into this algorithm to try to do everything safely. Understand the two women on that island are my sisters, and I'll blow everyone to Hell no matter who they are to get them back and be safe with them. I'm not trying to threaten you, but I'm not *not* trying to threaten you. I just need complete honesty from you. That's all I'm asking, and if you need to get out of that island and away from those people, this is the answer to your prayers. If you're defending them and want to be with them and believe them if they do, you will not leave this room."

Nieve nodded. "I understand and appreciate it. The only time I get to see my family is when I go to church, and their safety relies on me going back to that island. This has not been my favorite choice, but I feel like choosing to be with him is at least a choice. If you're telling me that someone is finally taking down the institution that creates that entire island, I'm going to help you however I can, but I need to make sure my family is safe."

Z looked through Nieve for a moment and then refocused. "So, you don't love him? Berkley?

"He's not the worst of them, if that's what you're trying to say. I do believe he cares about me. That being said, he hasn't done anything to protect anyone but my family and me, so I won't be throwing myself on a pyre for him. I'd love to see him survive, and maybe change who he surrounds himself with."

Z pushed forward. "How much do you know about how that island is defended?"

Nieve sat up straighter. "Well, actually, my uncle and my father, before he passed, were contractors that helped them set up the island. They used a lot of local people because of where the island is located. They needed connections with people who could make supplies happen, close and discreetly."

I saw a brief conflict in Zinny's eyes. This girl's family helped the island come to fruition, but now was not the moment to have a full-on jury trial deciding who was guilty and with what. Indy might be concerned with those kinds of things, but not Zinny.

"I need your uncle, and I need him now."

Nieve responded with all of her uncle's information. It looked like Lady Mafia was getting lucky...again.

INDY

Aster looked good. Thank God. She was somehow hooked up with one of the guys on the island, which didn't surprise me. People were drawn to Aster. It was partly why she might be the most dangerous of us all. Cain was in love with Aster. Wouldn't be the first to fall hard, and would only be the last if she chose it to be so.

The latest info from Z was that we would have intel on possible island defense systems, which I loved. Being able to put these bastards at a disadvantage was huge.

"Listen, I may need to get out there and let those meatheads find me so they can think Nieve is back where she belongs."

Aster squinted her eyes and then held out her arms. "I'd rather that we stayed together, but I get it. The more time they're not putting up the alarm for Nieve, the better. Berkely is not due back just yet."

I hugged her again. Happy that she was doing well and that she had her emergency medicine. "Stay safe. We're going to get out of this."

I ducked outside. As soon as I was off the steps, their lights turned off. Good. Protection was my main focus right now.

I made my way to the closest beach and started a slow meander. It took less than five minutes before I heard feet pounding up behind me. Caught. I was caught. Well, returned. I kept my head down and didn't make eye contact as I was hustled to Nieve and Berkley's place on the island. We had a bit more time, and from what I had heard from Aster, we needed it.

I closed the bedroom door and heard a dreaded sound. "Hey, babe! I'm home early. And my dick has been missing you!"

Shit.

CHAPTER
TWENTY-NINE

Zinny was focused, I'd give her that. The more time I spent with the Lady Mafia, the more I realized that they were each talented in different ways. To get good in this business, you needed a broad range of information about a lot of things. And Zinny had that in spades. While she discussed the defense plans with Nieve's uncle, it became clear that none of it was above her head. She understood how the defense of a land-mass was accomplished. From power supplies to guidance systems and weather maintenance, all of it is what she covered. The check-list in her head was impressive.

She spent some time with all the information laid out. A few times she chewed on her pen. Once she called me over to look with her at an entry point. And then finally, she had one last question. "Technically, these have small battery backups, so if the power was flipped off and stays off, how long do you think the battery power will last?"

"I told them to upgrade to the ocean salt batteries and have solar backups, and they were thinking about the expense of that, so in the interim I had the temporary battery backups installed. We haven't had a hurricane since those were in place, and as far as

I know, they haven't upgraded the system. So maybe three hours, max."

"So if the power is down for more than three hours, their defense systems will be offline and they'll only have the defense of the manpower they currently have on the island?" She tapped her chewed pen on the table.

"That's my prediction. Getting an exact time on a battery draining is messy business. Sometimes they last longer, sometimes they don't." The uncle shrugged his shoulders.

"I want a list of the things on the island that are the biggest power draw." She passed him an iPad. I watched as her gaze hardened. The plan was taking shape.

ASTER

I got a message from Z that I had to get as many things that run power going as soon as possible. Cain and I had a purpose now. We slipped out the back window, both of us dressed in all black to blend in with the night. By the time we crawled back through the window, the island's electric output had to have been multiplied by at least one hundred. All the girls I'd been talking to agreed to put on all of their appliances, hair tools, and lights. TVs were at top volume. Cain and I found every single thing that we could to turn on to make things worse. There was a device that monitored incoming ships that Cain was able to set to constant roaming. Air conditioning or heat in all the buildings was cranked up. Freezer doors where there was not high foot traffic had their doors left open.

When we got back to our place, we did the same. I messaged Z back, everything we could get a hold of had been turned on. We opted to be cold, and set the AC for eight degrees Fahrenheit.

"I think that'll do it. I mean, I think we covered every base." Cain slipped on another jacked instead of taking his off. I did the same.

Z's message pinged through again. "Indy is headed out to trip the power. Let me know how it goes. We had to pivot in the plan because Berkley got home."

"Indy okay?" Indy could fake out some security goons, but Berkley would very much notice that Nieve and Indy were different people entirely.

"She's good. Now has a captive. The timeframe for escape was just moved up considerably. You may have to notify anyone that you want to be saved. Mercy's crew is headed here now. They're willing to do transport." Zinny sent a little heart.

That small emoji told me more about Z's mindset than anything else. She never sent hearts. We were getting dangerous. More dangerous than ever before. I looked to Cain. "We've got to go back out and notify the girls."

"I have to make sure the old bomb shelter is open. Especially if they're cutting power." He rubbed his fingertips on his forehead.

"Divide and conquer, my friend." We opened the window to escape a second time. Indy was on her way to cut the power, I was going to try to save as many victims as I could, and Cain was being trusted to find us a safe spot to hide everyone.

A lot of things had to go right for this to go right, and that was making me nervous.

CHAPTER
THIRTY

I was running the comms, which was a hell of a job tonight. Mercy and his crew were coming through with transport to pick up the victims. And helicopters and a few small planes to bomb the ever-living bejeezus out of the island. It would not be a functioning space for human trafficking anymore by the time they were done with it.

I was worried about Indy, which kind of felt like being worried about a battleship. She could take care of herself and probably one hundred other people without breaking a sweat, but something felt off. Out of place. Off the tracks.

I was chalking it up to being a cog in the wheel of the plan here. That by not being in charge of the whole thing, I felt like I was missing pieces.

Mercy's first helicopter was due to pick up Zinny. Not me. I was going to be the point man with T in her aircraft as soon as they landed.

The comm that was marked for Indy buzzed.

"Yeah. Got you." I waited to see why she had radioed in.

"Well, I may have made things a touch harder."

I was relieved to hear her voice. "You make everything harder, Hot Stuff."

I heard her snort on the other end. "Berkley is now a prisoner in the basement of his house."

"Kidnapping men is really getting to be a selling point of a relationship with you." While we went back and forth, I typed, forwarding the information to everyone the web of comms attached me to.

"When you find something you're good at, you stick with it."

I bet she was winking. She was a winker. I missed the smell of her neck, the taste of her lips. As much fun as it was to flirt with her, we had a job to do.

"Tell me how this changes the timeline for you." I motioned for one of the men to come closer. When he was near, I pointed to my monitor. "Make sure Z has this information." He nodded once and set out.

I was pretty sure she had not only read my message but had processed it.

"We're letting everyone know that we only have a few hours. I'm not sure the time table on how often the outside guards check in on Berkley and Nieve. Could you ask our guest?" I was pretty sure I heard the clear ripping sound of duct tape. My girl doing what she did best. Taping men up. She seemed to make sure the arm hair was really caught in the adhesive good.

"For sure. You want to know what a typical night looks like at Berkley's place. I'll be back shortly."

I set my headset down and hustled to the room they were keeping Nieve and her uncle in. I didn't have to worry about persuading them to tell me the truth. After Z was done with them, they would have told me their darkest secrets, the pin number on their debit cards, anything.

Berkley's place would check in with security by 9AM, so Indy needed to make sure there was a way to clear security by then.

"Is it a verbal or visual check?" Indy was waiting for me when I got back.

"Most likely a simple text message, but they've been known to do verbal, and on super rare occasions, visual, in-person checks." I took a deep breath. That was a lot to contend with. I heard her blow out an exasperated sigh.

"Hey. You know, if Nieve and Berkley were experimenting with BDSM, he might be all duct taped up in bed." I wasn't sure if the logistics would allow this as an option, but I wanted to be some sort of help.

"You sexy genius. Love that for me. Thank you. How long do we have left?"

My chest swelled with pride, happy to be helping out the best I could. "Ten hours is my guess, by the time we have the choppers in the air and everything."

"How is that a lot and a little all at the same time?" She made a kissy noise and hung up without saying goodbye.

She was right. It seemed like forever but also, not nearly enough time to get everything done, like trying to move mountains as a scene change in a high school play. Never enough time to accomplish it.

ASTER

Cain was proving to be a very effective partner. We ducked into the bomb shelter after he picked the old lock. The metal door was rusted but sturdy. Inside was a mix of cave walls and drywall. The mildew smell was overwhelming, but it would one hundred percent be what I chose as a place to hide during a bombing.

"This will work. It'll be a tight squeeze if we can get all the girls, but I like it." I walked over to a work light and switched it on.

Cain also switched on a light and we both stared at the clump of bats that took off deeper into the cave.

That was not ideal. Even touching a bat could give you rabies, or at least that's what we had been told as kids when we used to hide in the caves behind one of our foster houses.

The girls started to trickle in. It was heartbreaking how good they were at sneaking and making themselves small. I was even more convinced that we were doing the right thing. We did a quick head count. We were missing three girls. The three I was hoping to see first through the door.

I messaged Indy.

> Hey, we have three girls that you need to make sure get here and let me know where you are on your procedures.

Her response was not what I was hoping for.

> Hey, so bad news. While I was doing my stuff, the cleaning lady came in and found Berkley, so we have to move even quicker. We still need 45 minutes of time to get the defenses off line.

I relayed the message to Cain. "I'm gonna have to go for the girls I think myself. I don't know where they are. You have to stay here and make sure that if all hell breaks loose you close this door."

I watched as his jaw clenched. "I'd prefer to come with you. Closing the door or something any of these girls can do."

I stepped closer to him. "Yeah, except we have to make sure they'll wait and close it after we're here. I'm afraid they would close it before we got back. It's what Zinny would do before we got back."

"From what you've told me about Zinny? She would have already thrown us out and then shut the door."

I nodded while leaning my head to the side. "Yeah, you're right about that, but we don't know. There are so many girls here. We could have a Zinny among us, so you stay and you open the door for me and the other three girls. And I want to make sure that Indy gets here as well. We have forty-five minutes to try to stretch this out."

Cain shook his head slowly. "You've got twenty minutes at best. We've got procedures and clearing the entire island takes less than twenty minutes on a good day with people alarmed as opposed to it just being a drill? They're probably doing fifteen." I took a moment to relay this to Indy.

She sent back a single word text.

Shit.

INDY

I went through all the stages of regret as I changed my outfit in the basement of Berkley's house. I found some dark colored Nieve clothes in the dryer, so I swapped out. The t-shirt was slightly damp, but I had no time. I hated that this plan had been rushed. I hated that the things we were concerned about and more were starting to unfold.

But I had to stow these emotions. Me doing everything I was good at was the most important thing right now. I needed to get Aster off this island. She had formed a bond with three girls, and they were her focus now. Get them to the cave. I needed to buy everyone time. As I hit the back door, I heard the door to the basement opening. They were sweeping the place.

As I walked out, I spotted a guard. He was scrolling on his phone, which was interesting to me. He should have been on high alert. I silently came up behind him. I was able to bring him down quietly. It was almost like I told him to sit on the ground using just the fingers on my right hand. He was boneless. I plucked his phone out of his hand and walked to the cover of a clump of trees. I called Z.

"What?" Her voice was crisp and clear like she had a headset on. I could hear the chopper sound. She was on her way.

"ETA?" Z would never turn around, I knew that. She would tell me that she would, but she would still come. Aster and I were everything to her.

"Thirty-five minutes. What's wrong?"

"I was made. I'm loose and Aster is getting three girls into the cave. Then they will be safe."

"Shit."

"I know. That's what I said. The power has to be off to turn off the missile defense of the island. Any other way to hold them off?"

I heard Zinny sigh. "I got the specs from the uncle. If the center missile is switched off, the rest follow."

"Okay. Sounds doable. What's the issue?" I stepped further into the clump of trees when I heard footsteps close by.

"The switch is on the missile. Underwater."

I turned to face the direction I knew the missiles were in.

"Fine. I'll go do that now."

"It's a long way down, like really far. You can't free dive that long." I could hear the engine change in the helicopter. Maybe they were closer now. I held the phone away from my ear, but I wasn't detecting the distinctive whop whop of the chopper.

"Can I get to it?" She knew what I was asking.

Would I be able to free dive long enough to get down to the switch? It was getting dire. I might not have time to worry about the travel time to escape.

"We can pull some evasive maneuvers. Just focus on getting the power to drain where you can."

"I'm not letting you get shot down. I'm just not. Sorry. You can change direction, or I'm going." I started navigating my path, staying close to the trees.

"If I turn around, you and Aster will be caught, and they will not be kind to those prisoners." She bit off her words.

"Then let's skip the fight and get to the solution. Tell me, Z. I'm going to do it with or without you. If you give me some hints, I'd really like that better." I shimmied down the side of a steep rock shelf.

"There are two palm trees that form a heart. Directly in front of them and out about 400 feet is a drop-off. It goes down far. Real far. They blocked off the water to build these fucking things. The center one has a yellow ring. You'll have to access the control panel and hit a combination and throw the switch."

"Okay. Got it. Tell Aster I love her. And get her the fuck off this island."

"This can't be happening." Zinny's voice was thick. She was starting to cry.

"I love you, Z. You're brave and amazing and perfect. Thank you for letting me do this." I ended the phone call before she could reply. I was all in now. Everything was resting on me. Zinny was the free diver of us all. I could hold my own, it was part of our training, but Zinny was like a damn mermaid.

I didn't tell her that drowning was not the way I wanted to go. It was the very last way I wanted to go.

I looked to my left and then to my right. The coast was clear. It was time. I stripped off my jeans and kicked off my sneakers. As I dove into the water, the baseball cap lifted from my head. I kicked as hard as I could. It was time to face a missile.

CHAPTER
THIRTY-ONE

I felt like my mind was screaming. These women had just sent Indy to her doom to save the girls on the island and every one of us in the helicopters.

I had a buzz in my ear. A very somber Zinny had directions for me.

"Your only job is to find her. Do you understand?"

"Yeah."

"It's gonna be her body, and you're going to get her and bring her to me."

"Copy. Bring Indy home."

I wiped a wet trail from my cheek. I shouldn't be surprised. I knew the type of life we lead was like this. Having Mercy, Havoc, and T with us made me feel invincible. Hell, these women made me feel invincible. I couldn't imagine that they were actual humans. That there were limits to what they could do. Breathing was a hard limit for everyone. Even Indy couldn't get away without breathing. It was surreal. It was a nightmare.

I just spotted land in the distance.

If I was still alive when we landed? Then I knew Indy wasn't anymore.

ASTER

Getting the girls to the cave required all the skills I could muster. I had to take down three separate guys that were guarding their cabana. I figured out why when I got inside. Jane was in labor. She was on her back, feet in the air. The other two girls were holding her ankles.

The midwife was there. She seemed to be an islander. She was calm and ready at Jane's business end.

"Ladies, we have to go."

The midwife spoke up, "This baby will be here in three, two, *push*!"

Jane leaned forward, somewhere else entirely in her eyes. The moan that came from her was as old as time itself. And then, in the middle of a life-threatening evacuation, I witnessed the miracle of birth.

It was stunning. First, there was no one, then there was a person. A baby. A red, screaming baby.

The midwife began to do things, cutting the cord, placing the baby on Jane's chest.

I scanned the room. The best we could do for a wheelchair would be the computer chair. I grabbed it.

"The missiles are going to defend the island, and if they don't, a crapton of armed helicopters are going to light this place up like a Christmas tree. We need to get to the bomb shelter."

God bless the midwife. I don't think there was a single thing I could have said to that woman that would have flustered her.

The midwife and the other pregnant girls helped me move Jane into the chair carefully. She was clutching her crying baby to her bosom. Sneaking this group to the cave would be almost impossible, but I wasn't leaving them. Midwife to the rescue again, she pulled out a walkie talkie and spoke in a different language.

She addressed me as if we were in a hospital and she was the head nurse. "We just need to get them on the front path, and my husband will be here with a cart. Then we can go to the bomb shelter."

That seemed doable. I wheeled Jane while the midwife packed a blanket between her legs. There still had to be the placenta to deliver. Jane wasn't really done with having her baby.

"Try her on your nipple." The midwife leaned over and pushed the baby's little mouth in the right direction. After swinging her little head a bit, the baby began latching on. Whether she got milk or not, it was keeping her quiet.

I was a little concerned that the midwife had spoken in a language I didn't know, which was rare, and hoping she didn't rat us all out. I had a good feeling about her deep inside. A large four wheeler with a flatbed pulled up. I was grateful when the midwife's husband hopped out and helped us transfer Jane to the cart. I hopped in the back with the midwife, and the other two girls crammed their pregnant selves in the passenger seat.

The midwife tended to Jane, comforting her when the baby gave up trying to nurse. "Let's let this one hold her and we'll get that placenta out. Allow the bumps in the road to help you. This will feel like passing another little head."

The sweet baby was in my arms and started a fierce protection emotion in my chest. The teeny nose. The soft skin. So precious. I could hear the choppers in the distance. I prayed we would make it in time. Before Zinny could unleash holy hell on the island.

ZINNY

Waiting to be blown out of the sky wasn't a feeling I was enjoying. It was pretty much overshadowed by my sinking feeling about Indy. The fact that she was giving her life for me, Aster, and every other victim on this island. I raged and mourned as the helicopters got close enough to land. A few went on. The alarms were up and we were taking fire now. I gave the signal to start small. I needed at least to know Aster was safe before I started Armageddon.

The com came to life. I could hear a door slamming in the background as Aster's heavy panting was interspersed with words. "We're in. I repeat, we are in."

I thought I heard a baby cry but refocused. "Heard. Prepare."

I radioed Mercy. "Fire away."

Maybe in the years ahead I would have flashbacks to what I did next. My spirit lifted from my body but was already on autopilot. I became what I was. A killing machine. Anyone that was even a hint of a threat was annihilated. By the time Mercy and Animal and their crews had circled back, I climbed into the remaining chopper. I scanned the horizon. No sign of Leto. No sign of Indy.

Aster was going to kill me for not saving Indy, and that was okay, because I kinda wanted to die.

ASTER

Cain was worth bringing for a lot of reasons. One of the strong ones because he knew where the emergency lanterns were. Midwife and husband were actually super decent people. They attended to Jane and the new baby like they had been working together doing the exact thing for years. We could hear the destruction around us. Because it was so encompassing, I knew it had to be Zinny and the Mercy crew.

Instead of fear, I looked around at all the girls crammed in the cave and saw hope. It was so beautiful it choked me up briefly. They had believed me and now we were a step closer to freedom.

I couldn't stop thinking about Indy. Her essence pounded my head. My heart.

I watched as the girls around me hugged and spoke softly to one another. They had such a bond. I was sorry they had experienced the trauma that had created that intense feeling, but grateful they had each other.

I sat down near the door, and Cain sat next to me. "You did it, Cupcake. You took on this whole damn island. Even if we're blown to smithereens, this place will be non-functional, and that's worth something."

I put my arm around his broad shoulders. "Thank you for sticking with me. How long do you think this will take?"

I waved a hand as the noise around us increased.

"A few hours. They won't want to move the girls until they're sure it's clean. It's a pretty big island, all things considered. We've got some time."

I switched it up and took his giant arm and slung it over my shoulders. I put my head on his chest as he settled his back against the wall.

"Wake me up when my sisters show up." Aster and Indy always joked about how I could sleep anywhere. They weren't wrong. The girls here were safe. Jane and her baby were getting all the things they needed with the help of the midwife and the first aid kit. I was going to think about Zinny and Indy and send them all my positive energy.

ON MY FIRST day of middle school, I was already angry. I didn't need the hormones of a teenager to make me mad. Life had been rough. I was in my seventh foster home. I was far past the cuteness of childhood. I was tall, stringy, and had a lot to say. I had a lot of emotional baggage and made sure I always had a fresh chip on my shoulder. Strike first. Don't answer questions.

The foster parents at this latest place had a few girls my age. They felt like I would be a good fit. They were hoping to make a bonded trio out of us. Like guinea pigs. I knew to look for two girls that had matching sweaters to mine. A green number with a clover on the corner. Apparently, foster grandma liked to knit for all the kids that passed through the house.

I tugged at it. It was itchy, but it had my name written in black ink carefully on the handmade tag sewn inside. That was the first time I had ever had something that thoughtful waiting for me at a home.

It was recess by the time I had all my paperwork in order. Another student walked with me out to the blacktop. I took the lay of the land. The kids were grouped up in clots. Cliques. The same old shit, different school. In the distance I saw the two other green sweaters sticking out like neon in the woods. My new foster siblings.

I walked up and the one with the brown hair gave me a quick nod. The other bounded up to me. "Zinny! I'm Aster. This is Indy."

I'd met girls like Aster before. Golden retriever style humans that never met a stranger. I shrugged. "What's up?"

Indy stepped closer. "Well, there's been a set of assholes bullying some of the girls over there by the playground."

I looked over. Four greasy looking high school aged guys were tossing rocks at a few girls.

I looked for the adults in charge, but the playground was just out of sight.

"They aren't supposed to be on that. It's the elementary

school's and it's closed down. The playground is condemned, but the girls like the swings."

One of the girls flinched as a rock hit her legs.

"Why don't you tell someone?" I leaned back and could make out a group of teachers talking in a circle.

"Then we all get in trouble for sneaking over to the playground," Aster answered.

I watched as Indy's fist closed and opened. "I hate this kind of shit."

I liked how much Indy cursed.

"We could end it," I suggested.

"How do you mean?" Aster narrowed her eyes as she looked at the boys.

"Bullies bully because they can bully. But if a set of bullies bully the bullies, well, that's just karma." I cracked my knuckles. My anger issues were ready to stretch their legs. It was always good to get in trouble on the first day anyway. Then you could have the benefit of a reputation. Watch out. I could hurt you. Don't even think of hurting me. It was a game, really.

"I like that idea." Indy leaned forward.

"They're bigger than us." Aster didn't seem reluctant, just practical.

"That's okay, we're foster kids. We're smarter and harder than them." I stopped at a clump of branches in the pile. "Let's get some wood."

Aster shook her head. "That's the 'put it down already' pile. When the boys find a stick, they have to..."

I attempted to finish the sentence for her, "Put it down already?"

"You got it." Aster winked and made me crack a smile at the use of the word 'tit'.

"Recess only has a few minutes left. Let's go." Indy strode over to the pile and grabbed a sturdy looking stick. Aster and I did the same. We headed toward the high school boys with purpose.

"Go for the legs. They have long arms." Indy struck first when the tallest boy tried to engage in conversation. She didn't even let him get a word out.

We might have been overrun by the bigger, more numerous bullies, but the other girls on the swing set saw their moment. They rushed the sticks and picked up their own.

In no time the boys that loved to hurt girls with stones were running off in the woods, cursing us all. The bell rang and we all chucked the sticks back in the put it down already pile. I walked into school with a smile on my face. Indy brushed her palms together to get the bark off of her hands.

"Well, that's how you do that, I guess."

Aster burst out laughing. "We're a Lady Mafia, kicking all the ass."

Indy wiggled her eyebrows. "Love it. Lady Mafia."

ASTER

When Zinny finally did the special knock to let me know it was her, I had already woken from my short cat nap. I checked on all the girls. They were freaked out but safe. They didn't know they were under our care now. That their lives would be their own. They would learn.

Cain swung the door open after I gave him the go-ahead. All I needed was one look at Zinny's face to know.

Indy was gone. I hung my head. I couldn't find it in me to believe. Zinny was broken, and that could only mean one thing. Our threesome was down to two.

ZINNY

Dread. It's funny that it was surprising me doing what we did. Taking the chances we took. I was always trying to escape the dread I was currently feeling. I knew it. Hell, with my childhood, it was damn near my first memory. Dread. What was next? Could I count on tomorrow holding still and just being normal? Or was I going to stuff all my belongings into a trash bag and get my world upended? But this was something more. It was why I trained as hard as I did. It was why I went as hard as I did. I believed I could keep Aster and Indy safe if I was at my best.

I knew that Indy felt the same way. Aster was more of a free spirit. Maybe she was the deadliest of us all. Hell, she played with a shellfish allergy just for the aesthetics.

I remembered following Indy with a stick to chase away the playground bullies. She and Aster were the first people to make perfect sense to me. To get me. To know that getting justice for the girls playing on the playground was an addicting feeling. And I always wanted more.

In my head I was the one that gave my life for the other two. I would actually joke that I would never see thirty and that they better remember me when they were in the nursing home together. Indy never laughed at that joke. Maybe she knew better. She knew it would be her.

Aster stood, head hanging down for a few beats. When she looked up, the tears on her cheeks glistened like tiny strings of a harp. She moved as if I had told her everything was fine. Other than the tears, she functioned. She rounded up the girls, checked on the girl with the baby, and moved toward getting them off the island.

She stepped over the dead bodies of the island security force like they were crumpled daisies. T had a team of boats on the northside of the island. The victims were escorted on. There they could choose from clothes and food and a few other comforts. T would take them all back to the mainland.

When they were off, Mercy, Animal, and Lock were hovering. "What do you need?"

Mercy's skull tattoo glistened in the tropical sun.

Aster was the first to respond. "I want the uncle here. We're going to comb the hell out of this place and find my sister."

Still the tears. But she was still moving. Still doing. I realized I had stopped doing anything other than slink near her.

Cain nodded. He wiped the tears off of her cheeks with his thumbs, but they were soon replaced. She couldn't stop crying.

I could feel myself hollowing out, like an old Halloween pumpkin left on a stoop far past the holidays. Just a shell. A hint. Barely holding it together. Ready to crumble.

Aster ran point. I wandered. I looked. I even did free diving once before the uncle got there and once after. It was long dark when it was time to give up. Indy was gone. Leto was gone. It made sense. The ocean was unforgiving. Leto was crazy about Indy. I wasn't sure he could swim, but I would bet my life that he jumped in looking for her.

I felt Aster walk up next to me after the last dive. She wrapped a blanket around my shoulders.

"Man, she's going to laugh at us when she gets back." She rubbed my shoulders and a chill shot through me. I looked at her in disbelief. The tears had stopped. In their place was a slightly delusional smile.

"Aster? Have you been snorting shrimp again?" I turned and faced her, the sand sifting under my bare feet.

"She's not dead. She'll be back. We just have to be ready when she is."

I saw that Aster was a pumpkin then, too. Just like me. Broken. Crumpled. But she was not aware that Halloween was long over.

Weeks. It was weeks before Aster and I moved on. We would check in on the island, scour the beaches. But nothing. We went over as much island security footage as we could, but the power outage and the decimation of the island had limited what we could see.

Aster was undaunted with the failure to find Indy's body or any trace of her. The last hint we had was the fact that I wasn't blown out of the sky. She'd manually reset the missiles.

Back on Mercy's compound, T was pressing us to make some decisions. Aster and I sat down with her on the back porch of our guest house. Aster and I hadn't even walked into Indy's room yet.

She passed us each an iPad with information on it. "So everyone has been given medical exams, access to therapy, and ways to get in touch with loved ones. Those who could be reunited were. Nix made sure everyone had a great cushion financially."

I scrolled through the names with matching pictures. So many people. So many women. It was really exceptional. A worthy cause. The loss of Indy was still singing my insides. I wasn't great at looking at the bigger picture. Aster touched each face—a small smile or a whispered name. But I wanted Indy back. Maybe that made me a bad person.

T leaned forward in her chair and set her elbows on the table. "On the next sheet, you'll find that we have a host of girls that are in limbo."

Aster looked up. "How do you mean?"

I could guess. Girls ran away when things were intolerable or dangerous. Not knowing that the world could be dangerous wherever they were. We had each other. The Lady Mafia. The three of us were our own support systems. We were lucky despite the fact that we had to be trained killers to survive. To protect each other. It would have been a lot harder alone.

"These girls were fed into the system and they've been spit out. They left for a reason and they don't want to return. Which I think we all understand." T clenched her jaw.

"We do." Aster set her iPad down.

T was a woman of few words, but the history flashed in her eyes. Pain. Loneliness. Hard choices.

"We all have some things in common then. With each other and with these girls." Aster started flipping through her iPad and pulled up a graphic design site. She started messing around on it.

"We do." T was looking at our surplus of people on her computer. "We have about twenty."

I peeked at Aster's iPad. She was designing a Lady Mafia logo. A cartoon girl with a gun.

"Who owns the island?" I was getting an idea. Maybe a stupid idea, but still.

T shook her head slightly at the change in the conversation. "Um, let me find out." She pushed away from the table and put her phone to her ear.

"What are you thinking of?" Aster put a high heel on her cartoon.

"That island. It's actually located in a pretty good spot. If we built on the place, we could have our own compound. Like Mercy here." I felt like I was betraying Indy by planning for something in the future, but I had to do something. Be something. Catch that feeling again—of making wrong things right.

Aster tilted her head and ran a finger along the gold chain she was wearing. "I'm listening."

"We could train these girls to fight like us." I pushed up from the table. Finding a purpose. Finding a way to take a breath of air around the pain.

"I like this." Aster bit her bottom lip. "But I met those girls. Not all of them will want to fight. Some want peace. Quiet. Healing."

"Okay. That's okay. We could just give them a place to stay. Where they are safe. They make their choices. Get an online degree. Learn some skills. Hell, something to put on a resume." I started pacing. This would be a huge project.

"When Indy gets back, she can run the money end of it. You can train the girls, and I can organize the peaceful side. It's perfect. Instead of the Lady Mafia disbanding, we can create a legacy.

There can be tons of Lady Mafia girls!" Aster came close and threw her arms around me. I hugged her in return.

If it wasn't for her complete delusion that Indy was alive, this would have been a great day. A good decision. A way to make the pain have at least a little purpose. I was worried about Aster because there would be a hard fall back to reality.

CHAPTER
THIRTY-TWO

The beeping was getting annoying. The dreams had been horrible. And amazing. And vivid. Most were water based. They were urgent. Sometimes all I could hear was my blood swishing in my ears. Sometimes I heard Leto's voice. Sometimes I just had ringing in my ears.

I knew I was dead, but the afterlife was disappointing. I mean, I had assumed Hell would be the spot for me, but I expected it to be like a waiting room. Or a devil. Maybe even a devil that loved drinking rum. In my head I'd called him Jack.

But instead, it was this blurry location mixed with sounds, smells, and memories. Sometimes I thought I could hear the waves.

It was time, though. I could tell it was passing. Like a nap that took too long. Like a hope that wasn't coming true.

The next stage was coming back. Being aware. I tried talking out loud more than a few times. Eventually, I made a moan. I could feel my fingers. The soft touch of a cloth on my face. The prick of a needle in my skin.

When I was finally able to open my eyes, I wasn't sure I was seeing anything.

A light came on beside me and a young man with a moon-shaped face gasped. "Oh. You're awake."

I watched him as he hustled around the room. It didn't look like Hell, and I felt far more aware than my dreams had been.

Something was in my nose. The young man was telling someone I was waking up or presenting with my eyes open. He turned on more lights.

Not sure why that terminology cleared my thoughts, but it did.

I was in a hospital? It didn't look like most hospitals I'd seen. It was more like a lovely hotel room.

I was looking at a doctor soon enough and a few more nurse type people. I began assessing my location. Last thing I remembered was... God I didn't know. How the hell I got here, why I was here—all of it was unknown.

I heard my heart rate's rhythm pick up on the audible monitor.

"She's getting agitated. Where's the guy?"

I started assessing my exits, locating weapons. I tried to see what was in my nose. I wasn't restrained, but I did have things attached to me.

"Hi, Indy. I'm Dr. Radcliff. Happy to see you. Try to take some slow, deep breaths. You're waking up after some time, so it'll be disorientating."

I dismissed Radcliff. He wasn't armed. I looked past him. There were four people in the room. The curtains were pulled tight, but I had a few exits to choose from. I couldn't figure out where I would run to once I got out of this bed.

Leto. Just before I was ready to rip the tube out of my nose and use it to choke out Radcliff, Leto was in front of me with the sweetest smile. "Hot damn. You're back. I can't believe it."

"Where?" My voice was rough from disuse.

He grabbed my hand. He knew right where it was under the sheet. He'd been here before. Done this exact thing before. He was practiced at it.

He quickly answered everything I was asking with that one word. "Hey, we're safe. Dr. Radcliff here has been taking good care of you. When I found you, you had ingested quite a bit of water. You've been in a medically induced coma while you healed."

I squeezed his hand hard. I wasn't sure where we were. My one question was, of course, about Z and Aster, but I didn't want to blow any cover or add suspicion. I guess I was skeptical from the jump.

He answered anyway. "I don't know, baby. We've had quite the trip. Most importantly, you need to know you're not alone, I'm here. And we're going to work really hard to get you up and back to yourself as soon as possible."

He was being cagey, trying to tell me he didn't know about Aster and Zinny. I focused on the doctor and his assessment, taking stock of what I had going for me.

I could move everything, it seemed. Time had definitely passed. How much time, I wasn't sure. Leto was laser-focused on me and that made me feel safer. He was a good wingman. Not as good as one of my girls, but I could trust him. God, I hoped my girls were okay.

I rested my head against the pillow. I was trying to retrace the injury that got me here. I let the island time rush back to me. Aster had been okay. Zinny had been incoming. Oh my gosh. The missiles. I had said goodbye. I locked eyes with Leto. He knew I had placed myself in the timeline of things that had happened.

I mouthed, "It was you?"

A small smirk pulled on his lips. I remembered failing to make it to the surface of the water. Of giving up. And Leto must have been around to pull me out. Things clicked. I reassessed. The curtains were drawn closed, so I couldn't make out what was going on beyond them. The people providing me health care seemed like the real deal. Their supplies were quality. If I had been in Mercy's hands, I could have already known what had happened to Zinny and Aster. T would have seen it, but I was guessing we were on someone else's compound. Maybe pirates. Successful pirates. If it was anyone that had anything to do with the island, both Leto and I would have been dead.

When Dr. Radcliff asked me to lean forward so he could listen to my heart, Leto stepped forward again.

"I'm in the room two down, so I heard the docs right away." He touched my hand.

Okay, so he was in the same building as I was. I understood. Bide my time. Be calm. Be still. We were still in this together. I was desperate to know how my girls were, but I had to wait. I refocused on the doctor while he checked my eyes.

LETO

When I got back to my room, I waited until I closed my door before I did a full-on dance. A big, hairy dance. The worry rolled off my shoulders like a log.

She was back. She was not only back, she was calculating. Planning. Concerned. Somehow it made my dick hard. Inappropriately, being that Indy was just barely awake. But I gave Leto Jr. a break because he was in love. Madly, overwhelmingly and wonderfully in love, and she was here.

Thank fuck.

I was hopeful. I was praying. I was afraid I was going to be wrong. I had planned out the rest of my miserable life without her. I was going to go to an island and live off the land until fate claimed me.

But I wasn't wrong. She was here.

"Hot damn." I was alone, but I had to say something to tell someone, so I told myself.

Literally everything changed. Instead of watching over her,

organizing her funeral in my head, my future had snuck up on me and kicked me in the balls. But in a wonderful way. A sack tap of pleasure. Okay, I was talking nonsense, but hope and relief had changed the tracks of my thought patterns.

Now I had to make sure she got everything she needed to thrive, to get better. And then together, we would get the hell out of here. I sat down on the bed and events of the island attack washed over me, now with tinges of miracles crowding in the edges. The sound of a helicopter landing outside set the soundtrack to the memory...

When I got to the water, I registered that the choppers were in the distance. If I could hear them and see them, that meant Indy was successful. I scanned the water. I never felt hopeless. The ocean had never been bigger in my life, but I saw her. I dove in and headed toward what had to be her, it had to be. I think I ripped out my heart and used it to manifest her.

She was going under when I got to her. She had been under maybe too long. I didn't let myself think about it. I treaded water near her until I could flip her into a rescue hold. The war on the island was in full swing. I forced myself to calm and then treaded enough to check on Indy. No breath. So pale. I tried to give her a rescue breath, but it was impossible. Instead, I focused on getting her to safety. Praying that being safe was still something that mattered when it came to Indy. The beach was filling up with security from the island. They wanted off. Like rats on a sinking ship, they would step on each other to stay above water. I pivoted and headed toward the dock. There was a speed boat, and I hyper lasered in on it. I had to let Indy go to pull myself in, and then grabbed her up before she could slip in too far. I yanked her aboard. I was exposed, but I didn't care. She was blue. Far too blue. I turned her on her side and then gave her a few real rescue breaths and a few chest compressions. I had never done them on a woman before. I tried to be gentle but firm. Before my brain could slip into complete frizz, Indy started coughing. It was the most beautiful sound in my life. I peeked over the side of the boat to see if the security forces were on to us. They weren't. I looked at the driver's side. The keys to the boat were just dangling there. I did a quick assessment. There were island security forces between me and the crew I came with. War was starting.

Indy was still breathing but clearly needed a hospital. I watched as the one on the island exploded. I used the explosion fallout to start the engine. The destruction of the large fireball hid me as I drove the boat into the night. We were escaping. I needed a few miracles to save the woman I loved.

The first two were already done. She survived and I found her. Next, I was going to have to get her to safety.

When I had enough nautical miles between us and the island, I cut the engine and settled next to Indy.

Her body was strong. She was still breathing, but I knew better. The brain could give up, give out, and the body could last for quite some time. I checked her heart rate and made sure her breathing was clear and easy.

I saw a bit of blood seeping out of her ear and I started to cry. I had to get her back to the mainland and soon. I used a few life-jackets to try to stabilize her position. I checked the instruments and pointed the boat in the right direction. When we go to the marina, we were not alone. I had no other choice. I had to dock the boat.

What I didn't expect was my brother. Matt whooped when he saw me. I grabbed his arm and pulled him toward the boat.

"Matt, why are you here? Never mind. Help me. We need an ambulance and..."

Matt winced and grimaced. "As much as I would love to help you, I'm sort of here with them." He used his thumb to motion over his shoulder.

I let my gaze shift to the other people on the docks. I didn't know why I assumed it had been Mercy's crew, but now that I was really taking them in, I knew they were strangers.

"You're with your captors?" I carefully lifted Indy into my arms. Matt reached forward and stabilized her neck, which was smart.

"Yeah. They got it in their heads that they wanted to get here

and take advantage of Mercy being busy and maybe catch the Lady Mafia."

My brother and I stepped out of the boat one at a time, with the smallest motions possible. Like Indy was a bomb.

"She needs care." I searched their faces.

"We got it." A tall man stepped forward and a smaller man sidestepped him. "This is Radcliff. He can help."

Matt leaned close. "He's the real deal. Super talented."

"Also a prisoner?" I held Indy close while Radcliff did an assessment.

"Yeah." Matt motioned for Indy and me to walk while Radcliff got her pulse rate. "Best to get her in the car."

He let go of Indy's neck and shoulders long enough to fling open the tailgate on the SUV. Radcliff suspended his assessment to help us slide her into the back of the vehicle.

"They just let you walk around?" I was still amazed that my brother was here, but I had to let the shock of that get pushed to the back of my mind. Indy's life depended on me staying focused and decisive.

"Yeah. I'm sort of like a pet. They let me do stuff."

Two drivers closed us in. Both were packing heat.

I had to abandon the conversation while I answered as many of Radcliff's questions as possible. He had one of the goons Matt was with get supplies from the hospital at the seaside town, and then we were on our way to another compound. Wherever Matt had been captive? I was getting to see that up close and personal.

I paced my room. She was awake. She was with me. All of her was in her gaze. While I had waited out Indy's recovery and reintroduction to her consciousness, I learned more about Matt's role in the Mariano crew.

They were mostly in Italy and Greece, but the place where they did business was near the edge of Morocco.

Matt had been killing it with his gambling and had been teaching the Mariano goons his ways. He was like a professor-level captive. Bitz was fond of him.

They were all pretty fond of him, which was hilarious and helpful. He told everyone Indy was his sister-in-law, a fib people surely believed with how devoted and destroyed I was with worry about Indy.

Because Matt was so well liked, I was provided a place to stay. I had leniency and Indy had Dr. Radcliff. He was a noted trauma surgeon before he was taken here by the Mariano family. They didn't let us have cell phones or contact with anyone, but we were well fed and sheltered, and most importantly, Indy had everything she needed to heal.

My brother and I had discussed a few times what to do when Indy got better. When, never if, I would want to get her back to Mercy's compound. I needed to find out what happened to the other members of the Lady Mafia.

I didn't want to rush Indy, and she'd just woken up, but we would have to move as soon as we could. Living here was dangerous, even if the family members were currently being tolerant. Anything could happen when you lived outside the law. We could very well get attacked, just like the trafficking island as retribution for something the Mariano family had done.

Time was barely on our side, so we did as much prepping as possible.

Matt said that once Indy was doing well, and walking, we could possibly hide in the bedding trolleys to get on a truck that took us to the next town over.

He was making decent money now with the Marianos, but he was ready to leave with me. It was the least he could do to thank Indy for saving him back in the casino.

I visited Indy as often as they let me. Dr. Radcliff insisted having me close was useful, and helpful for Indy's healing.

The day came when Indy and I returned from our stroll around the floor. We were alone. She leaned in close.

"I was able to get a peek at an iPad, and my girls are alive." She was glowing. Happy. Relieved.

"Did you get a message out?"

Indy with an iPad and some Wi-Fi could do some damage.

"No. Just got to do a basic search, but I was able to check the dark web on the service chat we had and someone had been talking with a client."

Indy stopped talking as a nurse walked in to get her vitals. This family had an entire hospital-like setup. X-rays, CT scans, surgery suites. It felt very much like a regular hospital stay.

Indy's vitals were amazing. Her heart rate was good, and being that she was low-key acting like a successful spy, it was time to take action.

That night when I left her, I whispered into her hair, "Be ready, baby."

I felt her head move in a nod as I kissed it. She would be ready. I knew it. I didn't have to tell her what was going down. I knew she would roll with the punches.

CHAPTER
THIRTY-THREE

Indy

I didn't sleep. Leto's warning to me was enough to keep my adrenaline spiked. I needed to get back home to Zinny and Aster. I'd been hoarding the weapons I'd been able to lift off guards and medical staff. I had a few scalpels and a small gun buried in my mattress. I had taken the opportunity to make sure they were at the edge of where I could reach them. My hand was semi in the crack, sheet pulled aside to allow me access. I had on bicycle shorts and a shirt under my hospital gown. Just little things I picked up on our walk around for my circulation. I had a pair of nurses' Crocs taped to the bottom of my bed frame.

Ready, I was ready. I had no idea how far away we were from the Mercy compound. The messages I spotted on the internet didn't give me any clues to where my girls were. I just knew once I was able to make contact, T would tell me.

Someone dropped a tray in the distance and I clenched the gun in my hands. I waited to hear an alarm or someone sounding scared, but there was just a soft curse. I hoped I was ready. I felt ready, but being injured and out of commission made me less confident. My brain felt foggy. I hoped my instincts would come in handy. To come this far and then not make it home? That was unacceptable.

I felt his presence first, then laid eyes on him. Leto was silhou-etted in my doorway. I grabbed my gun and scalpel. Matt was right behind Leto. He was dressed as if he worked here in the building, complete with a name badge. Leto held out his hand and I took it. Matt pulled two large carts filled with sheets in front of my room. They were linked together like a small train. Leto lifted me and set me in one like I was a kid in a grocery cart. I scrunched down and soon had my head covered.

Under the sheets, I could only assume what the noises I was hearing were. I stayed strung tight, ready to act if I had to.

An elevator. I stayed still. I was pretty sure a place like this would have cameras everywhere, so the fact that we had gotten this far was a miracle. It wasn't time to get out and make any noise.

I closed my eyes and tried to center myself. I felt the change when we were wheeled outside. The noise escalated, and I could hear machinery. I was liking less how much I had to trust Matt. Leto had earned my trust, but Matt was a wild card. The cart caught on some sort of lift and the cart I was in was pulled onto something else. The laundry truck, I was guessing. It would make sense.

Though, if I had a place like this, I would scan anything going in or out. When the doors closed, there were a few beats before Matt flung the sheets off my head.

He and Leto gave me support as I climbed out of the cart.

"We good?"

Leto gave me a closed-mouth smile. "Almost. We have the possibility of a search. Not regular, but if they are onto us in any way or we've been found out, when that door opens, it could be a bloodbath."

Leto had been in the cart with sheets and guns. While the truck bounced around, we armed ourselves. We pushed the carts around and then locked the wheels so we would have a type of cover. It wasn't bulletproof, but at least we weren't visual sitting ducks.

We felt the truck stop. The insulation on this storage trailer was light. We could hear everything. The guard and the driver were obviously friends. They went back and forth on what they had done over the weekend.

After what felt like forever, the truck rolled through the stop. We didn't get more than a mile before the truck came to a halt.

"It's time." Leto moved to the rolling door and threw the latch. He yanked open the door and Matt and I climbed out. When we came to stand, the driver of the truck was waiting, wide-eyed with a gun in his hand.

"They said you have to wait. Can't go anywhere."

I could tell the man was uncomfortable with a gun in his hand. The whole thing was slightly shaking.

Leto moved slowly with his hands up. "Listen, man, we don't want to hurt you. You sound like you had a great weekend. I want you to have more weekends."

The driver looked Leto up and down. "I want that, too."

Matt spoke up, "They want us because we are really danger-ous. If I were you, I'd just walk away. They can't fault you for that."

I watched as the driver let different futures form in his mind. He saw that we were also armed. He nodded once and set his gun down near his feet. "You know what? I really want to go on a hike. A nice, long hike."

The driver put his hands in the air and took off toward the woods.

We watched him for a few beats before Leto held out his hand. "How are you feeling?"

"I'm good." I was winded, actually, but we didn't have time to talk about it. He led me to the driver's side and Matt hoofed it for the passenger side. We were bumping along in the truck as fast as we could. When we rounded a turn, I saw that the laundry truck was leaking sheets and carts.

"I hope that slows them down." I pointed out the window.

Leto glanced and then put his attention back on the bumpy dirt road. "As soon as we can, we will switch out of this vehicle."

Matt spoke up, "We should've grabbed that guy's cell phone."

I gave us all a pass. "Yeah, we were just trying to get out of there. It's okay."

When we finally got to a paved road, Leto put the pedal to the floor. I was getting there. I was going to see my girls. I hoped they were okay.

ZINNY

We were on the island, Aster and I. The bombed out island was going to be legally ours. Mercy had a team of lawyers that were working on it for us. It would be totally redone. Lady Mafia would have a home, and Lady Mafia wouldn't die with Indy.

Aster and I had a camping tent set up. It was just us and the wreckage of the old place. There was wildlife now, and that was something we were looking forward to fostering as well. Maybe some rescue dogs and cats. The girls could help us with that. We had big dreams now. To be a place for the girls that didn't have one. That didn't fit in a box. We could train them and educate them. They would have everything they would need to protect themselves and pick their own future. It felt so right. I just wished Indy knew what we were doing.

Aster was still delusional. It was possible she would always be that way. She talked like Indy was coming back all the time. Cain, another collected guy, was smitten with Aster and willing to let her be as out of touch as she wanted to be.

T and I had talked about it more than once. That it was a protection mechanism. She would break without Indy. The three of us being a family was all that mattered to her.

We were out of touch on this island. Our phones didn't connect and the power grid had been blown to hell. Tomorrow, we were going to talk to Nieve's uncle. We kept Nieve safe. She was back with her family. I wasn't totally sure she was an innocent in it all, but I didn't have it in me to try to see her punished. Maybe losing Indy had made me soft.

When we heard the speedboat in the distance, we took cover. No one was slated to be here yet. Of course, a waterway could have boaters. That was part of the hobby, and in this part of the world, part of the trade.

Aster was wearing a bikini top and a sarong, with a knife tucked into the band. I had a pistol, as usual. However many men were in the speedboat, we could overpower them, especially when they were on the beach. I adjusted my sunglasses.

"She's back." Aster abandoned her coverage and stood in full sight. I stepped next to her. Whatever decision she made, I wouldn't leave her alone in it.

I felt my blood stop. Indy. It looked just like Indy.

Someone was pretending to be our dead friend. Everything in my head screamed danger, be wary, but my heart jumped to conclusions.

Aster took off running and I followed. It seemed like Leto was there. Yes, it was Leto. He was helping Indy up to the dock by the time we got there. Seeing Indy be unsteady was when I realized that it might be true. It might be her. My feet were glued to the wood.

Aster swooped Indy into a hug. "Where the hell have you been?"

Indy removed her sunglasses and waved me over. I lost all of my situational awareness as I stumbled over to my girls and hugged them both so hard. Explanations would come. I hadn't known that my soul had been in ruins until it slowly rebuilt itself.

Indy was here. Aster was here. Lady Mafia was reunited. I started to cry with my sisters and I squeezed them both to me.

EPILOGUE

ne year later

Waking up in Leto's arms was my favorite. We had the cabana doors flung wide open. The sunrise had happened a few hours ago, but we were taking a few minutes to celebrate. One year since setting foot back on this island. Thanks to him, I was rehabbed and strong. His brother, Matt, had returned to the Marianos and effectively bargained for Dr. Radcliff to visit his family again.

I ran a fingertip down the edge of his jaw. "You are still very handsome."

He let his smile show me his white teeth with the dimple that popped. "Glad you noticed. I set the handsome volume up to level ten to try to catch your attention."

"It's loud." I put my hand on his bare chest, letting my fingertips ruffle the hair there.

"Have to try to keep up with your gorgeous ass." He gave my bottom a light spank.

I laughed and put my head on his chest, listening to his heartbeat mix in with the sound of the waves.

"You excited about today? First group of Junior Lady Mafias?" He put a second pillow behind his head.

"Oh yeah. I hope the dynamics are good. It's a lot of personalities on an island." I traced the lines of his abs.

"You ladies can literally do anything you set your minds to. Even stay alive when you are supposed to be dead." He ran a hand through my hair.

"That's the truth." I let my hand dip lower, under the sheets. He was already ready for some fun times. "You're always up for some trouble, huh?"

"With you naked in my bed? Yeah. Twenty-four seven." He threaded his hand in my hair and guided my mouth to his.

Kissing in paradise, on the cusp of changing some lives, it had to be my favorite morning ever.

I took my excitement out on him, straddling his legs.

"Oh, that's the stuff." He started to roll his hips and I matched his rhythm. We weren't connected yet, but all his good stuff was rubbing against mine.

He reached up and started to play with my nipples.

"Hey, I love you, Indy." He stopped all movement. I looked down at his face. He had been all in as soon as I kidnapped him.

"Sometimes I kidnap the right people, I guess." I slipped a hand between us and rocked down on him. Once he was inside. I lifted up my hair so the light breeze from the ocean could cool me down while I rocked on top of him.

Leto put pressure on my clit, and it started to steal my breath. As I slowed, he increased his tempo.

"Hey, let me."

I unclamped my legs as he lifted me. When I was kneeling next to his hips, he sat up and ran a hand through my hair, fisting it at the nape of my neck.

"Did you hear me? I love you?" He got on his knees as well, leaning down close to my mouth.

"I heard you." I grasped him and cupped him, both my hands busy. "Now show me."

There was a low growl mixed with my name. Then he licked and nibbled my neck. "Mine. Mine. Mine."

He started rubbing me to the beat of his words, getting faster and faster. When I started to lose my balance, he dipped his other hand between my legs and pegged me with two fingers in my vagina and the other in the back.

"Fall for me, Indy."

I leaned toward him and my body weight was added to the pressure he was putting on me. The build was incredible. As I gasped his name, he slipped his tongue into my mouth.

"I can feel you coming around my fingers. Now do it to my dick."

Leto pulled away and my whole soul felt like a romance book being slammed shut right at the good part.

He manhandled me so I was on my knees on the bed. Leto entered me from behind and the book was open all over again. The font was bigger. There was matching music. He was an expert at me. As he went from one erogenous zone to the next, I realized that he had been studying me this whole time. Dreaming about this the whole time. My orgasm was a hit and he had been training as an assassin.

"Go." I gave him the only order I could verbalize.

Leto had been holding back. Going slowly. When he was totally inside me, I could almost feel him pulsating. He was big and determined. The noises we were making were borderline hilarious. He grabbed my hair and turned my head.

"Say you love me."

And even though I was tumbling in the middle of pleasure, my heart found a way to give him what he needed. "I love you, Leto."

His eyes went soft and he stilled. "Thank you."

"It's easy." I slammed back onto him. The fireworks of pleasure thrummed through us, my heart losing its borders to this man.

When we were both done with the aftershocks, he pulled me to him, spooning me.

Our breath got slower and our hearts stopped pounding. Cuddled naked in his arms was perfection. The smell of him made me happy. The heat of his skin was sealing this moment in my forever. He was mine, too. I had very few people in my world that I would die for. He was one of them.

We were all around a table on the island. We'd renamed it. We were going to pave it with success and freedom. There were ghosts here, but we would show them kindness and a little vengeance, too, if they required that.

We had new cabanas, places for girls and women to stay. We had a school and a training facility. It was everything we could hope for.

"We have a supply shipment getting flown in by T and Animal in about an hour." Zinny typed on her computer.

"Sounds good. Do we need to send anything back with them?" Aster typed on her computer.

I slid a file full of paperwork over. "These are some documents that I found yesterday that belong to the originals."

The originals. The girls we rescued. The first batch. A few wanted to come back and be on staff, but mostly T and Animal worked with the girls to get them jobs and a place to live. They had all the connections through Mercy's organization they wanted.

While sifting through an old file cabinet, I found some medical reports that seemed like they might be useful. I hated what this island used to be. Now? It had hope.

"Can we go over the inaugural group? I have an online doc we can all edit." I shared the document I was looking at with both Zinny and Aster.

I scrolled through the faces. We would get eighteen girls. Some had already been trafficked and rescued, some were homeless, and a few were from foster homes. When we were up and running, we hoped to have many more. I even had my eye on a few islands that were a short boat trip away.

I was mentally biting off more than we could currently chew, but that was okay. My insistence that the Lady Mafia had to disband after our last job had melted away when I hugged Zinny and Aster a year ago on the dock I could see from my window right now.

It was my final wall. I realized that now. I kept it up, and that insistence was keeping me from fully appreciating Zinny and Aster as my sisters, as my family. We could protect each other best when we were in each other's lives.

We discussed the girls on the page. Aster was focused on the girls that wanted to learn a trade. One wanted to be a chef, and the other wanted to learn how to fix cars.

I was interested in meeting the three girls that had STEM knowledge. One had required her foster home's alarm system to play music at 3AM. I wanted to get them tools and training to see what they could get into. I loved the idea of females infiltrating careers that normally boxed women out.

Zinny had a group of absolute troublemakers she was thrilled to meet. They were already brawlers, and she wanted to give them a reason and a season to throw a punch. Her grand plan was to get a few trained up to run our defense and offense programs.

I closed my computer.

Aster stood up. "Meeting over?"

She would be anxious to get back to Cain. He was a constant presence in her life. And he hated shrimp. He was really good for her, preferring her natural looks over the allergic reaction.

"Not yet." I stood as well and Zinny joined in. "I think we need a toast."

I went to the mini fridge and pulled out a bottle of champagne. Aster went to the cabinet and got out three glasses.

Zinny sat on the table and waited while I popped the cork. Aster held out the glasses, and once they were all half full, I set the bottle down and we surrounded Zinny.

I held up my glass. "To my girls. I love you both so much. I'd do anything for you, and deciding to stay together here on this island has made me so, so happy."

Aster smiled at me. "Thank you for staying alive and coming back."

Zinny touched her glass to both of ours, making a soft clink. "Lady Mafia."

Thank you for reading Lady Mafia! I hope you fell in love with the ladies as much as I did. Please enjoy this free, extended scene.

Join Aster, Zinny and Indy as they return the ring to Aster's evil ex-boyfriend.
Plug this address into your browser: https://BookHip.com/ MWXTDTF Or point your phone's camera here:

ALSO BY DEBRA ANASTASIA

WHAT TO READ NEXT...

Coming of Age

DROWNING IN STARS

Mafia Romance

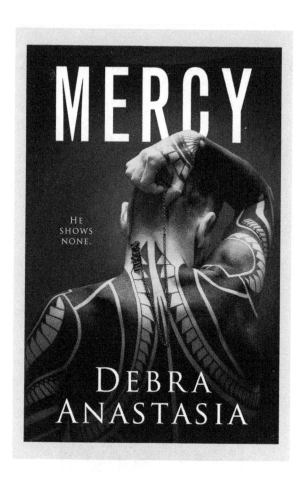

MERCY

Paranormal. Standalone with kick ass female

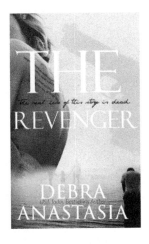

THE REVENGER

ACKNOWLEDGMENTS

A huge thanks to you, the reader. I'm back again with another story and it is always humbling to know that I will find you letting it into your heart. My sincerest thanks.

To my beautiful family, T, J and D, I absolutely adore you and am so proud of all of you. Thank you for putting up with me.

A HUGE shout out to my parents, Steve and Valerie who support me everyday from Florida and care for me and my sister like we still live in their house. We got the very best. Thank you for encouraging us and making (good) examples out of yourselves.

Pam (The original Indy/Zinny) and Jim! Thanks for keeping my bedroom ready in NY I love you. To Jim's mom Cathy, you are incredible.

Helena Hunting, Lady Mafia member for life

Tijan, Lady Mafia member for life

Mom and Dad D, You are sunshine and gold

All my Beta Beauties! Michele, Marty and Brandi, Amanda, Tessa, Carol S, Chantell, Jennifer, LLL, Sara, Melissa, Elaine, Jenni, Jenny, Heather Brown Jeananne Elaine! You are an emergency swat time of awesome.

Debra's Daredevils! We've been doing this for so long, I am the luckiest. Bloggers, 'Tokkers and 'Grammers! Thank you so much for continuing to ride this train with me. I'm honored.

Whole Brower Literary Crew— Kimberly Brower , Amiee Ashcraft and Joy Thank you so much for everything!

Aunt Jo and Uncle Ted—you guys are so cool thank you for being so supportive and amazing.

BLACKBERRY the talking cat, thank you for all the directions given to me with a look of disdain. I had no idea how often you needed treats.

Bud: Erika— CVS forever, Jenn, Kelly B, Ashley S, LLL, Sarah Pie, Melissa, Ashley, Christina love you guys!

Cassie S thank you so much for all your help

Paige Smith Editing— You are such a gift and make me laugh and keep me from waffling. You are the best.

ABOUT THE AUTHOR

Debra creates pretend people in her head and paints them on the giant, beautiful canvas of your imagination. She has a Bachelor of Science degree in political science and writes new adult angst and romantic comedies. She lives in Maryland with her husband and two amazing children. She doesn't trust mannequins, but does trust bears. Also, her chunky tuxedo cat talks with communication buttons. So that's fun. DebraAnastasia.com for more information.

Pretty please review this book if you enjoyed it. It is one of the very best ways to support indy authors. Thank you!

Scan the code on the next page to stay connected to Debra:

tiktok.com/@debraanastasia
facebook.com/debra.anastasia
instagram.com/debra_anastasia

MY DAD

FREE BOOK PLATES

Okay Daredevils. I have literally the cutest offer ever for you. My dad makes my swag down in Florida. He is freaking adorable about it and is very serious about his job. If you want a FREE signed bookplate(s) email my dad and we will send them to you and whatever swag he can fit in the envelope.

To receive an envelope sealed with adorableness and extreme efficiency email: debraanastasiaDad@gmail.com with your full name and mailing address (plus how many bookplates you need!!)